A NEW HOPE

An anthology of fiction and poetry, giving a voice to young people.

Will Maslen - Neve McRavey - James McGunnigle

Emma Taylor - Gabriel Gontor

Calum's Legacy

Published in 2021 by Calum's Legacy Books

ISBN Paperback: 978-1-7397518-0-7
Ebook: 978-1-7397518-1-4

Published with the help of Indie Authors World
www.indieauthorsworld.com

Dedicated to Calum

And to Eddie, who didn't see this published.

Introduction

Calum Sinclair Macleod died on 12th October 2007 after contracting meningitis. He was three months short of his 13th birthday. Calum was our son.

He was a bright, inquisitive, funny, kind and friendly boy who was loved by all those who knew him. We wanted to remember Calum in way that helped to express who he was, promoting fun, friendship and co-operation.

Through Calum's Legacy, Indie Authors World funded five young people aged 16–25 from Central Scotland to co-author, publish and print a book. Will, Neve, James, Emma and Gabriel took full ownership of the writing, editing, design, production and print processes with support from the expert team at Indie Authors World. They grew in skills and confidence; developing and honing their creative, entrepreneurial and teamwork abilities to emerge at the end the process with their own book, published under the Calum's Legacy imprint, printed and ready to bring to market.

Becoming a published author is a transformational experience for many, opening doors, establishing or raising profiles, boosting confidence, connecting with peers and generating an income stream. We launched Calum's Legacy to enable young people, who may be otherwise lacking in creative and entrepreneurial opportunities due to their situation or responsibilities, to experience that positive transformation at first hand.

The five came from different backgrounds, some more experienced writers than others. Together they bonded into a group of supportive friends, helping each other with the problems they faced. The result is the book you hold in your hand.

The process took longer than we had hoped as COVID interrupted our plans but the young people stuck with it.

The four novellas and collection of poems cover a variety of genres. Will's story is a modern fantasy about the spirit of a sphinx. Neve delves into the witch trials of Scotland's past by giving it a contemporary twist. James writes a humorous fantasy that has echoes of the nonsense verse of Edward Lear and the comedy of the Goons. Emma's poetry is both personal and poignant. Gabriel's incredible imagination delivers a high fantasy tale of dragons and swords. Each of them has faced their own personal challenges to deliver these wonderful stories and poems.

The title of the book comes from Calum's love of Star Wars, and seems appropriate as hope must come from giving young people a voice.

We hope you enjoy these stories.
Sinclair, Kim and Kirsten Macleod

For more information:
Instagram: instagram.com/calums_legacy/
https://www.indieauthorsworld.com/calums-legacy/

Acknowledgments

Our thanks to everyone who supported our project.

The authors who have helped fund it by publishing books with us.

The mentors who gave time and advice: Claire Duffy; Caroline Johnstone; Eddie Doody; andClaire Miller

Cue and Review for the use of their premises.

Those who donated cash and laptops for us to use including Graham Forsyth, Ian Pilbeam, Robert and Jane Melvin, Eddie Doody and Caroline Johnstone.

Jane Melvin for feeding us, our young writers especially loved your cakes.

Ann Roberts for her giving her time and support to the group.

Anne Macintosh and business gateway East Dunbartonshire for support and encouragement.

Helen Cochrane for a training session on illustration.

Alasdair Currie of XYZ for the design of Calum's Legacy Logo.

Christine McPherson for her help in editing some of the work.

The
Sphinx
Will
Maslen

1

In a dim corner of my room for longer than
my fancy thinks
A beautiful and silent Sphinx has watched me
through the shifting gloom.

Adam had been stretching out the time it took him to enter his flat from his office each day for a few weeks by that point. Generally this meant following the cluster of his colleagues down to the pub round the corner, or wandering around the scum-covered pond a little further down the road, or standing in the newsagents staring into the freezer until he thought of something to buy. Sometimes, it was a combination of all three. Whatever he did usually, it certainly came as a surprise to him when, one grey Tuesday, he found himself in the cold, echoing halls of the local museum. He had never been overly interested in museums. The stale, papery smell of old taxidermy and stone was sharply familiar and made him think of his long, dull, embarrassed school days as he pushed open the heavy holly panelling of the door.

The light inside was dim, his feet were sore and he could just as easily, so he kept telling himself, turn around and head for his usual evening drink. But somehow, there he was all the same, letting the door swing shut and echo in a whisper through the quiet, stone entrance hall.

The building had always been a museum, erected in more profitable times; its grand arched halls now seemed to swallow light, as well as many of its own exhibitions. Warm dusty shadows rested over twisting marble statues, frozen insects, warped and gaping mammals leaking sawdust, pottery with lightning bolts of plaster down their ancient sides. Adam vaguely recalled hearing talk of the museum trying to raise funds to stay open; clearly, so far, it had successfully clung to life, though he'd heard little of it since.

He paused at a display of ornate globes, feeling awkward at how loudly his stiff shoes echoed on the tiles. In the dim orange light the globes sat like plump cantaloupes. He peered down at sea serpents churning up half-imagined seas. Adam couldn't help but think the little plastic sign jutting out from beneath the display didn't tell him much, just the year the globes were made (which was painted in swirling letters on each base anyway) and a few brief sentences which seemed only to describe what they had on them. There was colourful lettering beneath this that suggested you try and point out a few countries you recognised, he assumed it was aimed at children.

Adam looked briefly around him. A bored-looking attendee in her late fifties leant against the entrance way, and an old man in a raindrop-studded tweed cap was wandering absent-mindedly by the oil paintings along the far wall. It was hard to imagine children coming here. Hard to imagine anyone, really. Once again he thought of turning around and heading for the pub, the dull monotony that came with talking to people who didn't quite care enough to leave the conversation, but had no interest in taking it further. It wasn't a huge leap from the half-hearted information laid out for him on the museum's little plaques. His eyes continued to wander, coming to rest on a large yellow banner above a set of closed double doors to his right:

VISITING US FROM LONDON

UNLOCK THE SECRETS OF THE IONIAN SPHINX

Adam checked his watch; he figured the place would be closing soon, but he might as well take a peek. As if he didn't feel silly enough, his heart picked up a strange pace as he headed toward the sign. He switched the hand that held his briefcase and shouldered open the door onto a much smaller room than the one behind him.

Weatherworn pillars and hunks of carved stone lurked close to the ground beneath a set of tall arched windows. A glass display case or two showed painfully delicate-looking licks of silver and gold, shards of jewellery and the tools of their long-dead crafters.

In the centre of the room, the stone haunches of a lion jutted. Adam slowly walked around to the head of the sphinx. She was hewn in crisp, clean, curving lines out of a light, sandy stone. Wings were folded close to her body at each side; her face was nestled in what seemed to be a mane of feathers. It was a strange face. Her head was tilted backwards slightly and her eyes were serenely closed, as if she were basking in the sun. A gentle smile tweaked the corners of her lips. She lay with her great paws stretched out in front of her. *Life-sized* Adam thought to himself, but then there was nothing for her to be a life-sized version of.

The sign beside her read that she had been discovered on an island in the Ionian Sea that spent the majority of the time largely submerged in water. Few other signs of life were on the island, and the leading theory was that the sphinx had once been part of a cargo that had found itself beached there by some happenstance. Her appearance and whatever technique had been used to make her matched no specific culture that was known of. Like the Great Sphinx in Egypt, she had wings and a lion's body, and her mane might at certain angles resemble a Nemes headdress like those seen on depictions of pharaohs, but she was clearly female despite her feathery mane which aligned more, the sign explained, with a Greek interpretation.

Around the sphinx, other shipwrecked and curious items were placed, evidently the curator had been trying to lean into the fun mystery of the display. Adam looked at the strange round eye of a sea urchin, the tangles of dried seaweed and jars of pickled fish, the bits of china and ivory cases worn into soft, organic shapes and then he turned again to the clean sharp lines of the sphinx. She didn't look like she had come from the sea.

The old man in the tweed cap entered the way Adam had come. Still seeming reluctant to stray far from the walls, he smiled amiably at Adam from over the sphinx's head, and after pausing to examine a set of jasmine charms, moved on through another door. Adam looked again at the face of the sphinx. Two impossibly blue eyes stared calmly back at him.

2

*… And let me touch those curving claws of yellow
ivory and grasp
The tail that like a monstrous Asp coils round
your heavy velvet paws!*

"Please don't be dramatic."

The sphinx kept her luminous eyes on him as she spoke. Her voice was soft and fluting, and a low rumbling seemed to come from deep within her as she spoke each word.

Adam's briefcase had skittered into a display cabinet and sprung open with a frightening clatter, sending a half-eaten packet of crisps from his lunch and several papers flying. Adam himself was also sprawled on the floor, staring up at the sphinx in horror. She stood up and stretched, her wings spreading taught as eight curling scythes for claws unsheathed themselves with luxurious slowness.

Adam made a soft choking sound. The sphinx yawned, a glint of teeth in shadow, and settled back down on her pedestal, crossing her front paws. "I am rather dependent on you remaining composed."

"What?" said Adam.

"Your composure. I need you to keep it."

"You're alive," said Adam.

"Yes, I am alive."

"Um..." said Adam, his hands clammy with sweat. "Well..." Adam could think of nothing more to say and left his mouth quivering for a few moments. He shook himself. "I have to go," Adam decided. He scrambled to his feet and started shovelling papers and broken bits of crisps back into his bag.

"Please don't go, I need you."

Adam stopped short; he swallowed, and glanced over his shoulder. The sphinx looked almost small from back here, under the dusty grandiosity of the museum's high ceiling. He made a mental note of this as evidence he was becoming unhinged, certainly it had been a growing concern over the past few years. The sphinx's blue eyes were still fixed on him. Huge, burning, cold blue eyes.

"What?" said Adam again. "I want to get out of here. I need to go home." Adam began shaking his head. "Bloody hell," he muttered to himself, mashing in the last sheet of paper and slamming his briefcase closed. "*I'm* going home to take a nap, it's the stress, it must be - I've not been right in a while, I should call..."

He straightened so fast that he stumbled backwards, then pivoted to face the monster warily. He couldn't think of who he should call.

Adam gave a little jump as the sphinx rose to her full height. "Haha!" he cried, voice rising into a hysterical squeak as he shook his head again. "No thank you. Don't do that please. Should I call an ambulance? Would that be too crazy? Have I gone crazy? Please stop moving around like that..."

"Didn't you come here to escape?" The manic smile that was beginning to spread slipped from Adam's face. The sphinx jumped down from her perch, blocking the main exit. "I could smell it on you the moment you walked in here or I would not have said a word. You want to get out of here. I can help you."

Adam shifted his weight from one foot to the other, running his hand through his hair. It unnerved him that someone, or something, could see into him so easily. "What do you care?"

He watched with fascination as the sphinx sat back on her haunches. Her monochrome colour meant that each position she took seemed static, unmovable – and yet she moved. Joints rolled and muscles pulled beneath the thick, uniform smoothness of her hide. Her mane ruffled when she turned her head, but as soon as she was still, she once more was nothing but stone. The thought of her moving again was somehow ridiculous, so every time she did so, it was a surprise.

The soft, fluting voice spoke again. "I was not made to be here. The place I watch over has been calling to me for millennia; if I do not go soon I will forget what I am for, and that is a terrible thing for a creature such as me. I am not like you; my course and my purpose are fixed, perfect. I am a being of honour, and I know my cause – if you help me, I will help you, that is the way of such things."

The sphinx licked her lips. "There's a storage cabinet set into the display base behind you that is currently empty, and large enough to fit you inside if you curl yourself up tightly. The guards will come around at closing time, " (here, Adam snorted at the use of the term 'guards',) "and then all goes quiet, the overhead light leaves us and nothing moves until morning – except one guard, who is slower than the others and more comfortable; he will not come here for plenty of time and even then only cast his point of light about the floor like he is pretending it is a frightened mouse."

Adam looked at the doors behind her. His heart, which had been misbehaving since before he even came to this blasted room, was fluttering like a butterfly in his ribs. He knew there were sensible, reasonable responses to this situation. He knew, but all he could find was a strange, wondrous excitement rising in his chest, like he hadn't felt in a long time. It was slowly dawning on him he would do anything not to let the feeling go.

"I will give the signal as soon as the big light leaves us," the sphinx continued, "and you will open the latch to the window which I cannot grip, for while I was blessed by many things in my creation, thumbs were not one of them - and I shall fly us out of the window. Then I shall owe you my freedom and fulfil my debt by giving you yours."

"Where would I even go? What freedom?"

The sphinx grinned, revealing a set of shark-like teeth. "What do you yearn for? You dream of escape, so you must know you are not free. Where do you dream of?"

Adam shifted from one foot to the other. His palms were sweating, he couldn't believe he was genuinely considering this. If he thought too hard the spell would break, the restless drive in him would turn to fear, he could feel it teetering there in panic.

"I don't know! Somewhere sunny where I could drink all day and no one would be able to bother me."

The sphinx took on a thoughtful look. Her strange eyes glittered as she regarded him, as if calculating the sum of his parts. "I believe I could fetch you to what you seek."

Adam passed his hand over his face. Then he rubbed his fingers through his hair. "Can I..." He squinted at the impossible creature before him. "Can I just like... touch your paw or something? I'll believe you and I'll do it or whatever you want... I just... I need to know I'm not seeing this. By myself, I mean. I need to know you're real."

The sphinx paused, then extended a tufted paw. Her claws were politely tucked away, but their ends still lurked in full view, they looked very sharp. Adam stepped forward and reached out his hand. She felt rough as sand, and cold to the touch, not soft with fur as he'd expected - if he had expected to feel anything. He dropped his hand quickly. After his initial shock, he'd been waiting for a true reaction, or perhaps some kind of clarity, like he'd suddenly understand what was going on.

But all he could do was keep staring at the impossible being before him, and the only clarity he had was the strange new singing thrill in his chest. The touch was a mark against the hallucination theory. He wasn't sure if he was more horrified by the idea he was mad or that this thing was actually standing before him. He wanted to ask for another go, he wanted to ask a lot of things. Frankly, he wanted to start crying.

As no new thoughts came, and nothing was revealed, Adam found his body simply carrying out what the sphinx had sugges-ted. He disposed of his briefcase in a shadowy corner of the room, then crawled on his hands and knees into the unlocked cabinet base while the sphinx settled into her usual pose on her pedestal behind him. Though he swore quietly as he knocked his head, and again as he twisted his hip, the same wandering, desperate spirit that had warded him longer and longer from his own apartment each day, now had him tight in its grip, and would not let him say another word.

~

Adam did indeed fit into the cabinet, but the sphinx had failed to mention the discomfort of the situation, or how long exactly he would have to wait. He didn't dare move around or try and find out how much time had really passed, but with each agonising second, the pressure on his neck, back, hips, knees and ribs were building until he was afraid that even once the sphinx signalled for him to get out, he wouldn't be able to unknot his body from the abstract ball it had now become. From his position, curled on his back with his head propped against one corner and his knees squeezing the air from his chest, he could see a thin sliver of yellow light that was the cabinet door. He wondered where his colleagues would be now, where he would be if he had gone with them. Somehow, this situation still felt like a step up; there was no room in the cupboard for the restless loneliness that a few beers and a boring conversation seemed to agitate in him.

At one point, he heard a woman calling in the distance that the museum was closing and to exit the building. Shortly afterwards, he heard a door open and close, presumably a staff member checking for stragglers. Another aeon passed, and then suddenly he was plunged into complete darkness.

There was a soft thump, and Adam assumed the sphinx had jumped down off her perch. Then came the loud scraping sound of a curved claw running down the cabinet door. Adam had been thinking only of the discomfort he was feeling and the thrumming in his chest. The horrible rumble of the sphinx's claw awoke him like a bucket of ice water, and fear gripped his stomach. *What was he doing?!* He had clearly gone insane. If he wasn't hallucinating, then the thing on the other side of the door had definitely got him alone so it could eat him. He'd practically marinated himself, he'd trussed himself up without a second thought! In his mind he plunged for the exit sign, but he was sure she was faster than him. Maybe he could create some kind of distraction?!

The scratching sound came again.

"Please don't eat me!" Adam blurted out unintentionally. A soft chuckle came from outside the cabinet.

"I depend on you to leave this place."

"How do I know that as soon as I leave this bloody cupboard you're not going to have yourself an Adam buffet?!"

"Adam?"

"Yeah that's me," Adam said bitterly.

The sphinx's voice rumbled through the wood. She must have been leaning on the cabinet now. "You can call me Anat. We are both trapped in here. The main door is locked from the outside. The window is the only option and in that, you have the 'upper hand' as it were." The sphinx chuckled softly at her own pun. "I need to go home, and I need you to help me; it would be useless, if not unpleasant, to eat you."

"*Or*," replied Adam, "you have no interest in leaving your sweet gig as a museum exhibit enticing the odd passers-by into a cupboard and saving them for a late night snack." He was angry at how much his voice seemed to be breaking. "This is crazy. This is a crazy thing to be doing right now. I can't believe you just admitted you'd enjoy it!"

The sphinx sighed. "I could easily break this cupboard open and prise you from it, devouring your tender flesh, if that would better fulfil your expectations, though I find bending fate to the will of men rather tiresome. Would it bring comfort if I gave you a riddle?"

"A what?"

"A riddle. The power of tradition might bind us better than my honesty."

Adam snorted. "Are you for real?"

"We have been over this Adam, I am most real. I know many riddles as I am rather fond of them, though I embarrass myself to be perceived like my siblings. However, I might give you a riddle and you might take as long as you please to answer it, and meanwhile we can be on our way."

"I mean, it's all well and good but I still only have your word don't I? I really hate riddles. I *hate* riddles! I hate *this*! When does the bloody security guard get here?!"

The cabinet door creaked and Adam thought he could see a slither of eye through the little gap. "If you try to call for a guard I shall have to let out a breath unto your hiding place, and you will find yourself sliding sweet and soft into a sleep from which you may never wake up."

"What?" Adam squeaked.

"I have means of killing you while you are inside the cupboard Adam. You may as well leave it and walk with the fate you have already chosen."

"You're bluffing!"

The now rather musty air in the cabinet was suddenly disturbed by a wonderful, lilac-scented breeze. Almost instantly, Adam began to feel lightheaded. He scrabbled at the door until he felt the weight outside it pull away and he rolled himself gracelessly onto the floor, sucking in great lungfuls of cool and welcoming dust-filled air, his lips still buzzing from whatever strange toxin he had just inhaled.

"Okay. You got me," he grumbled, and sat up to meet his fate.

3

A thousand weary centuries are thine
while I have hardly seen
Some twenty summers cast their green for
Autumn's gaudy liveries.

The room seemed much brighter than the inside of the cupboard, though the only sources of light came from the buzzing green glow of the emergency exit signs and the smudged streetlights outside beyond the fogged glass.

"Quickly," the sphinx whispered. Adam found his eyes locked on her once more. What had been eerily beautiful in the light became a fresh source of horror in the dark. Her uniform colour blended with the shadows so it was as if she had simply risen from the floor, or knitted herself together out of thin air. Her face hung like the moon. Adam shuddered at her eyes. They threw back the green glow of the exit sign as if lit from within. What had been a patchwork quilt of bird, lion and woman was now something else, something complete. Nothing about her was entirely anything at all; she was something new, serene, incomprehensible, terrifying...

"Adam! Quickly please. The window."

Anat lowered her head and took a step forward as she spoke, causing Adam to not so much snap away from his thoughts as jump from them. He hurried to the window, almost scrabbling at the frame before he stopped and told himself to take a breath and look at the damn thing.

The window was very tall and slender, with metal grating in a fishnet formation over its bubbled glass surface. It looked like it would be a tight squeeze for either of them, made tighter still by its awkward height above the dust-clogged radiator. There was a simple iron handle on the side of the window frame with a keyhole below to keep it locked in place. Adam swallowed and grasped at it, fearing it wouldn't turn, but it moved easily in his hand - whoever had shut it last had forgotten to lock it.

Adam briefly wondered if the sphinx had taken note of all these circumstances, and if so, how long she'd been waiting to take this chance. To his embarrassment, he found himself briefly hurt by the concept of her choosing him more out of circumstance, than some innate value she sensed in him. The sound of traffic and cool, busy smells of the city at night came rushing into the room as he pulled the window open. He paused, waiting again for something to go wrong - an alarm to go off. Something.

Nothing stirred. He was about to break out of a museum with one of its display pieces. He flinched at a movement from out the corner of his eye, unable to bring himself to look at the shadowy sphinx again. He was being broken out of a museum *by* one of its displays. He could feel his pulse thundering in his fingers, between his ribs, everywhere.

"Shall we?"

"Wait! I should get rid of evidence. My briefcase - "

"It is done. I already ate it."

Now Adam did look at the sphinx. "You *what?!*"

"It seemed to contain nothing of importance."

Adam scoffed, "It was *my* briefcase! You ate my briefcase!"

"You don't own anything really, not that you can let go of with such ease."

"I was hiding it! For safekeeping! And you - "

"We must fly now, Adam. We must hurry."

"I don't - " Adam looked out of the window, realising that the side of the building they were on meant a drop to the ground that must have been over seven metres. He could just make out the pavement below. Adam swore quietly, "I can't bloody fly!"

Anat pushed past him, her rough skin scraping his shin even through his trouser leg. "Of course not," she snapped, "I shall carry you."

Adam looked down at her doubtfully. She was perhaps large enough to take his weight, but he sincerely doubted they would both fit through the window. To his surprise, instead of pausing and letting him clamber onto her back, Anat leapt lightly onto the sill, then disappeared into the night.

"Wait!" Adam leaned out of the window; Anat was standing on the empty pavement below. She seemed to be one with the concrete under the yellow wash of the streetlights nearby - the window opened onto a dead-end alley that was often used for illegal parking. Right now it was empty, but people were walking past occasionally on the main street just a few metres away. Partygoers for the most part, by the sound of it. If they happened to glance down the alley...

"Are you coming?"

"You want me to jump? I thought you were carrying me!"

She was too far away to know for sure, but Adam swore the sphinx rolled her eyes. "I'll catch you! First you must jump."

"This is bloody insane," Adam said to himself, but he already had a foot up on the windowsill. The breeze picked up again. He felt a wave of dizziness come over him as he shifted his weight onto the narrow ledge, making the mistake of keeping his eyes on the sphinx, on the ground, which now seemed to stretch with the grandiose height of a cliff edge down to the violent sea. "I hate heights!" Adam tried to call, but his voice broke into a squeak.

"Just jump!" the sphinx called back.

Adam was about to point out she might not catch him when he heard a noise from the room behind. Slowly, his head still spinning from his perch, Adam twisted his spine to peer into the dimness. The security guard made an odd, guttural sound of surprise, like he was choking. His flashlight lurched and Adam, blinded and terrified, found himself falling backwards into the cold rush of the night.

4

But you can read the Hieroglyphs on the
great sandstone obelisks,
And you have talked with Basilisks, and you
have looked on Hippogriffs.

Instead of hitting the ground however, Adam felt the cloth of his jacket yanked tight. Something was gripping firmly to the fabric between his shoulder blades, so that he swung hunched, legs flailing in the rushing air as he rose higher and higher. He tried to gasp but the wind snatched his breath away, he couldn't even cry out. Below him the city was a blur of coloured lights. His body kept bracing for the impact that never came. They swung upwards, wind rushing, towards the hills that could be seen above the western suburbs of the city.

By now, he had figured out the sphinx was carrying him. His new fear came from being seen. What would people do if they saw a man being carried off by a sphinx? Maybe they'd mistake her for a giant bird. He wondered who you would call to deal with such a thing. Animal control? The police? The army? Everything seemed so silly now. All these names and professions, as if anyone could really prepare for anything, could do anything at all in a world where sphinxes fled museums.

Perhaps it was too dark to see them, perhaps some strange power kept attention at bay, but for whatever reason, within moments they were ghosting over dark, rustling fields and Adam had not seen a single upturned face. Trees sighed as they passed over, cattle lowed to each other in the cool night air. Occasionally they passed over roads, and as they reached the soft swell of the hills, sometimes he caught sight of long passenger trains and streaking cars that glowed in the distance like deep-sea fish.

He tried to speak many times but the wind seemed to snatch his voice and fling it far behind them, leaving him breathless and frustrated. His fingers and toes had gone completely numb and the pain from the pull of the fabric under his arms was escalating faster each moment. Suddenly, to his horror, hills fell away on each side of them and the impossibly vast, black maw of the ocean opened up the horizon - they were headed straight for it.

"I can't do this!" Adam yelled, but the wind snatched his voice and flung it far behind them. He could see the waves breaking across the shoreline now, they would be over deep water in a matter of seconds. A wild panic came over him and he kicked out, twisting in Anat's grasp. He felt the sphinx clench and then came a tearing sound. Then with a jolt the dark shore was rushing towards him and the wind was rushing upward through his hair. He didn't even fully register he was falling, just felt the shock of a sudden change as the ground spun closer and closer.

Pain exploded in his sides and he lurched upwards again, screaming out in agony. The world glided under him for a few more moments before the sand caught him explosively and he rolled to a breathless and blessed stop.

A breeze across his face as he sat up, groaning, announced the landing of the sphinx. She frowned down at him. "What on earth was that for? You are worse than a fish, writhing around like that! I might have dashed your brains and then where would my honour be? Very much the wrong kind of freedom to seek!"

Adam was busy examining the almost ribboned, blood-stained shirt and tender scores down his side. He hissed between his teeth. "I was in pain! I knew I wouldn't make it over the sea."

Anat twitched her wings in a frustrated motion. "You were quite safe, and would have remained so out to sea."

"Yes, but I was in *pain* Anat! I can't travel like that! You could have warned me! And now my sides are sore."

"Pah! Pain is a mortal thing's game. It is just a little scratch, because I had to catch you in a rush! Because you were stupid!"

Adam groaned again and leaned back into the ground. It was a cool, clear night, the stars above blinked coldly. He took in a deep breath. Everything ached from the strangeness of the past few hours alone, and the sea air was fresh and soothing in his lungs. It had been ages since he'd been to the beach, he loved beaches.

"Pah," the sphinx repeated to herself again quietly. Adam heard her pad away a few paces and then lie down. When he sat up again, he found her facing away from him, staring out at the horizon. There was a faint orange glow to their left that might have been the dying remnants of the sun or might have been light pollution, he couldn't tell. "I need to keep going," Anat said softly. Adam was surprised to hear the same pleading in her voice as in the museum when he had tried to walk away.

"Okay." Adam ran his hand through his hair and followed her gaze out to sea, it was a lovely night. "Okay... if pain isn't a thing for you that's fine. But it is for me, I can't do that again." He paused, thinking. "Could I like, ride on your back?"

The sphinx turned her strange eyes on him and kept them there for a long time. "Hm. That is inconvenient for me - it will slow us down, I cannot fly so well."

"Well, hanging by my shirt collar is inconvenient for *me*, so it's only fair you take a turn." For once, Anat didn't seem to have a reply. "Pretty please?"

Anat tilted her head. "I know that one, but I have always wanted to know what makes the please more pretty when you whine."

"Aw c'mon Anat! Just let me this once." He clasped his hands together and nudged her gently, then paused, weighing up how wise it was to wheedle to a sphinx. "It would stop me whining."

Anat grumbled softly under her breath; Adam was pretty sure he heard the words, 'Eating you would stop it also,' but he wasn't going to push the matter. Finally, giving a mighty sigh, she crouched down and stretched out her wings. "Not in many thousands of years, perhaps millennia, has a human had such an honour, and you seem too foolish to take note of it, so it is wasted. Please do not get your legs near my wings, I need to move them."

Adam repressed the urge to punch the air and carefully clambered onto the sphinx's lean back. It didn't feel as secure as he had hoped, but it was still better than dangling. "Where should I put my hands?" he asked after a moment of awkward waving.

"Clasp them about my neck, but if you tug at me, I will be displeased."

His confidence in the situation fading rapidly at every moment, Adam leaned forward between Anat's narrow, feline shoulder blades and clasped his hands at her collar. Without another word, Anat started to move forward, building into a run along the shore. Her wings unfurled on either side and then with an upward push that Adam could feel thrumming through him, they were soaring through the air.

From his new perspective Adam could appreciate just how impressive it was that the sphinx flew. Her hide was rough and unyielding, the cold lion's body he now desperately clung to felt heavy and hard and yet the wind was carrying her like a seabird. She kept her wings outstretched, the barest twitch adjusting their direction. Occasionally the wind would suddenly change and with a mighty flap, she would send them spiralling up to catch a new draft and then they would glide on. There was something ceaseless and unmovable about her, even in the open air. He wanted to ask what she was made for, but he knew the wind would take his voice. Around them the ocean stretched out forever and the stars wheeled. The cold air was merciless, and he kept his face pressed against her coarse mane in an effort to hide from it. With no landmarks but the unmoving stars, the first few moments of flight seemed to stretch on endlessly. Without realising it, Adam drifted off to sleep.

5

And the priests cursed you with shrill psalms as
in your claws you seized their snake
And crept away with it to slake your passion by
the shuddering palms.

When he woke up, it was to find sunlight streaking the sky. The sea threw the light back at him, painfully bright. Feeble, wind-swept clouds interrupted the rays so that the light came down in great buttery slabs and slanting pillars, turning the vast landscape into the echoing memory of a ruined church. He was silent for a while, taking in the view.

"Where are we?" he yelled into the wind eventually.

The sphinx, bright as fresh straw in the clean morning air, turned her head. "What?" she yelled back over her shoulder.

"Where *are* we?"

"Close!"

Adam nodded to himself. He wondered how much of a grasp the sphinx had on geography, and what she was using to guide her way.

The sun climbed higher as they flew. Adam discovered if he clenched his legs together and was careful, he could unclasp his hands and sit upright, flexing his numb fingers. Anat's back seemed to warm in the sun like stone, so that she almost felt like a normal living thing.

His first clue they were nearing their destination was a gull wheeling past them, laughing to itself. As they continued, more appeared, clustering close to the waves, but they swooped upwards and scattered around them as the sphinx passed overhead. Rocky crags began to rear their heads, breaking the water into white foam below. Then, in the distance, a whole island.

It looked like it had been torn straight out of a travel magazine. Lush green foliage brimmed over a perfect white shore. Its borders spidered out craggily in different directions, the ocean frothing against coral rocks in places, and being soothed into hushed green lagoons in others. He spied a stream bleeding out into the ocean on one side. It was lovely; he laughed with the seagulls as Anat dipped down to meet it.

6

He came along the riverbank like some tall
galley argent-sailed,
He strode across the waters, mailed in beauty,
and the waters sank.

"A volcanic island," the sphinx said as they walked along the shore. "The rock might still be hot in places, but it is generally safe." The green fringing the beach rolled upwards in staggered cliffs. Here and there, the bare face of black stone could be seen. The heat was unbelievable. The sand shimmered so that Adam half expected waves to steam as they hit the shore. He had already stripped off his torn jacket and sweated through his ragged shirt. The air had a thick, dewed heaviness to it that carried the smell of vegetation and salt water like perfume. Everything was so bright it hurt his eyes; he squinted into the tree line, but the change of light was too drastic to make anything out.

Adam cleared his throat. "I could use a drink now, to be honest Anat. Please," he added as an afterthought.

"Ah yes." Anat's tail twitched as she took the lead. "Fear not, I have remembered. It was a display near me once you know. 'The *human body can become dehydrated and die in a heated environment in a matter of hours'."*

They rounded a small outcrop and the sound of a bubbling stream rose over the gentle waves. Clear water carved sleek, snaking lines into the sand before them, throwing back the light into Adams eyes. All the same, he could see tiny grains of sand...

"Is it clean?" he asked, suspiciously. He was certain this time Anat rolled her eyes.

"This way."

Adam groaned and rolled back his head. His tongue had the taste and texture of a rotting toad on hot tarmac. He could barely see for the sunlight, and he was losing all his precious fluid from his armpits. When he looked back - and his eyes had cleared their swimming motion from the movement - he was alone on the beach. He blinked, he hadn't heard her move away. Panic gripped at him. "Anat?" he called out, hating the high ring of his voice in the emptiness.

Relief rushed in with the sound of the waves as Anat's head emerged from the foliage. "Are you not coming?"

"I didn't know where you'd gone!" Adam approached her meekly. Her face disappeared into the greenery once more, following the gurgling sound of the stream. The undergrowth seemed to swallow it, so he could only sometimes see the snaking glimmer of water in the dappled light. All around, he could hear strange calls and rustling. At one point he lost his footing, threw his palm against a slimy trunk to steady himself, and a lizard leapt out from between his fingers where it had been disturbed from its camouflage and scampered away. He had been too tired to be proud of not screeching.

The trees stopped a few metres short to watch as they came to a dripping face of black volcanic rock. The water was gushing from an open wound just above their heads, crowned by thirsty vines that reached for it. It tumbled prettily down the tapered stone, frothing wildly in places and gurgling peacefully in others.

"This water has filtered through the rock, it is the cleanest you will find."

Adam had barely heard the second half of Anat's sentence; he was already scooping mouthfuls of the clear, cold, wonderful liquid into his mouth. Then he just let the fall cascade over his face, his mouth wide open and his eyes screwed shut. In that moment, it was the best thing he'd ever tasted.

~

"... Crap." Adam cautiously shuffled himself up off the bank of dead coral the tide had revealed on its way out, gratefully planting his feet on soft sand, a jagged stick clasped in one hand.

"What?" The sphinx was sprawled on the shore nearby.

"I was trying to catch dinner and I got... this fish."

"That's s'posed to happen," said the sphinx; her voice had the lazy disinterest of someone now on their third hour of soaking up sun on a white shore.

"Bloody look at it!" said Adam. Having now reached her side, he brandished his stick at her. The fish flopped at its tip, still gasping slightly. It had the vivid colours of a parakeet, and fins that ended in lovely streaks like dovetails. "Do you have any bloody idea what it is?"

The sphinx opened one blue eye and cast it benignly over the fish. Adam felt a sudden twist of anxiety in his stomach. Over the course of the day, he had become increasingly more comfortable around the sphinx, but with each new line of familiarity he crossed, came the fear he had pushed it too far.

"It is a fish," she told him. "I hardly know which kind. I don't care to know all other species by name and virtue."

"I don't bloody either! What if this is the last one? What if I just hunted it to extinction!? We're - what - near Hawaii? Maybe? Everyone says we're fucking over Hawaii. I can't believe it. I'm helping to fuck over Hawaii... Oh god... what have I done...?" Adam clutched the stick in both hands, staring in despair at the now mostly still animal as he gently knelt by the sphinx. "I'm never eating a tuna crunch again, I don't deserve it..." At this point, Adam abruptly stopped talking, as he had realised a life on the island meant a life without tuna crunches anyway.

"If we are near Hawaii, I have never bothered to learn such things. I read at the museum once that a quarter of the fish discovered there are found nowhere else on Earth. I have been all over the world and I have seen fishes like that before many times," Anat decided.

"That's cool," said Adam dully. He leaned back on his haunches and twirled the stick. "I dunno if it's okay to eat though."

"What do you mean?"

"It might be like... poisonous."

"I'll eat it."

If the sphinx had pressed, Adam would have admitted he had never gutted a fish and didn't like the thought, and that he rarely cooked fish at home. In fact, that his main experiences with fish involved tuna crunches and trips to the chippy, and that having felt the disgusting give of his stick and the horrifying flail of the fish his appetite had suddenly disappeared. As it was, he just despondently jerked the thing off his makeshift spear by the tail and tossed it to Anat.

Watching her eat was a harrowing reminder of the fact she wasn't human, so he turned his gaze back out to sea. His mind wandered briefly back to his empty flat. It was the weekend, he was pretty sure. He doubted anyone would have even noticed he was gone yet.

They had already travelled the circumference of the island and through to its tallest peak with the express purpose of seeing how cold and how still it was for Adam, who had been suddenly loudly worried about volcano eruptions. They had also found several nice clearings for building shelter and gone into its only cave, which Adam had expressed concern over, mostly because of his dim memory of the events in *Lord of the Flies*.

The sun was not quite setting over a calm, pearly sea. It had deepened into a yolky orange and was dripping lovely colours into the pale water. The evening would have been idyllic, should have been, but all Adam could feel was the weakness of his hungry limbs and the horrible itch of thousands of swarming insects that were attacking him any time he came in from the water's edge. He stared despondently at the blue shadows in the sand, flicking at them with his stick. "Maybe I should try and get a fire going."

To his surprise, the sphinx raised her head and looked at him with interest. "It's been many years since I have seen a fire."

Adam laughed, secretly relieved to have something new to talk about. "It might be a few more yet, I've not tried making one from scratch since I was in Scouts."

7

You kissed his mouth with mouths of flame:
you made the horned god your own:
You stood behind him on his throne: you called
him by his secret name.

Anat stared intently into the leaping flames. Adam had never seen the expression she had on her face, a weary curiosity. It struck him he'd never seen her look unsure about something. He nursed the secret pleasure that he was able to throw her, even a little, along with the cool liquid in the itching husk of coconut in his hands as the sky slowly deepened its hue and insect chirrups rose into a twilight chorus.

The scene before him looked like a painting. The sphinx's sandy colour took on the flickering flush the fire threw at her. Twin flames danced in the depths of her blue eyes. The world faded gently to black around her. Above, the trees made a sharp silhouette over the rich, cool jewel tones of the sky. His mind wandered back briefly to a poem he had read some time in high school, about a sphinx and dramatic scenery. The smell of burning firewood and the almost sweet, gentle flavour of coconut water were nearly as rich as the rum he would have added if he could. He didn't notice he was smiling.

"You don't want to stay here, do you?"

Adam dropped his gaze to the crumbling silhouettes of burning wood. "Hm?"

"You have complained all day, and frankly I fear for your survival. I forget that many humans have distanced themselves from the sensibilities of the wild."

"...I guess... it would be a little freaky just being left out here. I seriously don't even know how I got this coconut." "I fetched it for you."

"I tried reaching it for *ages* and then it just dropped right into my hands! Can you imagine?"

"You scrabbled half-heartedly at the tree for a bit and then came and whined at me most childishly until I went up and passed it to you."

Despite her teasing tone, Adam found himself suddenly ashamed. He spoke a little unevenly around the knot of his stomach, hoping she would notice his words more than his voice. "It really just goes to show how much hard work pays off." He forced his shoulders to relax, catching hold of joviality once more. "But who's to say I'll be able to do it again?"

"I feel you are trying to avoid the crux of the matter."

Adam sighed and looked up, feeling a little jolted, as ever, when he found Anat was looking at him steadily. She didn't seem annoyed. "I guess." He hated the defeat in his voice.

"What shall we do to solve this riddle then?"

"Will you take me somewhere else? Could you?"

"I would not be fulfilling our agreement if I did not."

Adam wasn't sure if that was true but chose not to press the subject. "Where else could you take me?"

"Somewhere with no one 'to bother you', somewhere you might have food and shelter... I believe I can think of such a place, though it is further out than I have taken you so far."

Adam shifted uncomfortably. "Will you be okay getting where you need to go after?"

"I have waited over eighty years. I'm sure I can wait a little longer."

Adam didn't know what to say to that. He kept his eyes on the fire until his coconut husk was scraped clean and the flickering shadows and distant, sighing water lulled him into a fitful sleep.

~

He was rudely awoken by sunlight before the evening's fire had even gone cold. The insects had been busy in the night, and he was freckled with mosquito bites. He swore something wriggling came loose when he brushed a hand though his hair. Everything was aching from the hard ground he had lain on.

Adam half staggered down the beach, leaving a trail of tattered clothes behind him and wondering vaguely about his last malaria jag. The ocean was blessedly cool against his skin, bites and sunburn and all. He hadn't swum in years. As a kid, the pool always made him feel too exposed. He'd hated being in the changing room with the other boys, the smell of festering chlorine and the hard, slimy tiles. He'd always loved the beach though. He swam up and down the shoreline for a bit and then just lay on his back and drifted until thirst drove him back inland. He washed himself thoroughly under the little waterfall, tipping his head back to drink.

When he got back to camp, he found Anat staring at the sky, her tail twitching, the green and brown speckled bulges of two unopened coconuts at her side. She spoke without turning her head. "The wind seems good for us. We should leave soon. Can you think of a way of carrying these?"

He ended up bundling them into a huge, umbrella-shaped leaf and tying the whole thing together with a torn strip from the remains of his shirt. He felt rather pleased with himself; maybe he was better at survival than his first day on the island would have anyone believe. When he looked up to grin at Anat though, she was still impatiently twitching her tail and staring at the sky. "What are they for, anyway?" he asked.

"For you to eat and to drink. We will be flying for a long time."

Adam swallowed. He hadn't really let himself think about yet another leg of the journey, or what it might do to him. His stomach was already starting to feel the effects of his strange, minimal diet over the past day, his body felt worn in a way it had never done before. The scars from where Anat caught him mid-fall were already stinging, but somewhat ignorable scabs at his side. He had no idea what would happen if he got properly injured or sick. He had no idea what he would do if he got properly injured or ill while he was alone. Adam shook away the thought. "How long do you think? Can I go on your back again?"

Anat turned her head a little to give him the side eye. "If we leave now and the wind stays kind, not accounting for any moments of rest or relief your flesh might need, we can make it there by dawn tomorrow."

That didn't sound so bad. Adam clapped his hands together brightly like he was trying to kickstart a boring presentation at work. "Best get started then!"

8

*Foul snake and speckled adder with their young
ones crawl from stone to stone
For ruined is the house and prone the great
rose-marble monolith!*

They stopped a few times on their journey, but only long enough for Adam to relieve himself and stretch, and hack the outer shell from his supplies with a sharp stone. For the second coconut, he felt so weak from the journey, he had to get help from Anat.

For the most part, their stops were on rocky crags or sand dunes that hissed softly out from under the tide. Near the end though, Adam got to cast his eyes around wide plains, young woodland and the distant lights of civilisation. Neither of them were eager to extend the trip, Adam never wandered off to explore.

He slept once again through the last few hours of flying. This time he awoke to tall, grey mountaintops blushing orange under the rising sun, dusted here and there with snow, starkly shadowed beneath and around them against the slanted light.

He could see green foliage and gushing water in the deep crevasses and valleys far below. Once or twice, a huge scowling bird of prey swooped past or glided with them for a while, cocking its head at the strange sight. They were intimidating to say the least; Adam had the brief thought that the image of him in his tattered clothes, riding a sphinx through a sunrise surrounded by raptors was approaching what you'd expect to see spray painted on the side of a van. He was just missing a wizard hat, or maybe he'd be a large-chested woman instead. Adam laughed out loud, and kept laughing for a long time, high from the thrill.

It wasn't until Anat twisted around in a gut-wrenchingly tight circle that Adam noticed the cluster of houses below them. The village was nothing more than a grey strip of concrete cresting the slopes over a forest-clogged valley, lined with the ramshackle patchwork of civilian homes. Anat continued her circling, lower and lower. Adam started to panic, not knowing why she was leaving herself so exposed to the inhabitants, but after a few passes, he realised he could see no movement in the town. Several rooftops seemed to be crumbling, and as Anat coasted along the street into a smooth trot, he noted the woodland below swallowing the cracked, disused road and beginning to spill from windows and back yards.

9

The god is scattered here and there: deep
hidden in the windy sand
I saw his giant granite hand still clenched in
impotent despair.

The ghost town had everything he could need. It was as if the inhabitants, a practical lot by the looks of things, had simply got up and walked away into the forest one day. Tinned food still lined the shelves of the single, dust-caked shop. Books on camping and wildlife survival, maps of the area and handy tools he might need were abundant - wherever they were, it had once been a hub for hikers. He would be able to learn how to survive in comfort long before supplies ran out. Most of the buildings were in disrepair, but there was certainly plenty of shelter, places where he could build camp, even generators he could attempt to work with. Each turn revealed a new welcoming gift, and worsened the glum, sinking dread that had begun to build in the pit of his stomach.

"What do you think happened to this place?" he finally asked, a little gruffly. They were ferrying things he might need to a hopeful-looking two storey house he had picked out about halfway down the street - the exact centre of town. He was

"

carrying a case full of bottles, an extremely exciting find, but a heavy one.

"Hm?" Anat was padding along beside him.

"All the people."

"Oh. People are always rather temporary, especially in places like this. I expect the town no longer wanted to be found."

Adam shuddered. Anat's relationship with the world seemed to revolve around strange, forgotten places. He had been nursing a growing fear that this was what had drawn her to him in the museum. "What if it doesn't want me?"

She smiled up at him, revealing the inhuman points of her teeth in her gentle, human face. "One little man won't disturb anything. You'll be gone in the blink of an eye to these mountains, to even this laid stone."

She was trying to tease him, he realised. Somehow, her humour didn't make him feel better. He looked down the hill to the green depths of the valley. In the distance if he strained his ears, he could hear the sound of rushing water. He shifted the weight of the crate in his arms, trying to give some relief to his aching fingers. "Do you think anyone will remember me?"

He could see out of the corner of his eye that Anat was still looking at him, her grin gone again as quickly as it had come. He kept his gaze fixed on the invisible horizon. "I'll remember you." He was surprised by the sincerity in her voice. She seemed to wait to see how he would respond, but he couldn't think of a good reply. Anat pressed on in an odd, jovial tone he hadn't heard her use before.

"A sphinx's memory is a wondrous thing. Truly, it is an honour to be remembered by a sphinx. We are the stone keepers of the secrets of this world, we watch over knowledge, nurse it through the feeble throes of mortality and give it new meaning in the eye of forever. You won't need to care much to be remembered by anyone else, my memory is worth that of a thousand lives."

Adam had to laugh at that, it came out sounding more bitter than he'd intended. They stopped at the battered screen door. Adam set the crate down heavily by the front step, stood and stretched, his back cracking. "Is that why you were made?" he asked suddenly.

The sphinx tilted her head. "In a sense."

"What do you mean?"

"It's hard to... explain in words. I guess that is the thing. I am a man-made image. I was put here to say something that it would be hard to say any other way. It is... limiting however, to have such a singular, unchanging purpose. I suppose part of what makes humans so interesting is that they can forget."

Adam sat down on the front step and scrubbed his hands over his face. He didn't want to go inside - it was cold and smelled of mildew.

"I shall leave you soon, I would like to take flight before the sun sets once more."

Adam looked up at her. "Are you sure? I feel like I should do more to thank you. Maybe we could climb up the hillside a bit and have a toast to our journey, you know? Make a proper goodbye of it..."

Anats' expression was unreadable. "It *has* been many years since I have tasted mead or wine." she said eventually.

"Well," Adam grinned, lifting a glass bottle out of the crate and tilting up the label for her to read, "I hope you're up for trying beer."

~

Adam found a pack of oat tea biscuits and ate them between breaths as they climbed, stopping sometimes, and trying to disguise his panting by turning around to the view. It really was spectacular. The sun bathed everything in gold, so that Anat blended into the rock as she leapt around the narrow path, seeming to enjoy the altitude and terrain. Adam had to wonder if her home had similar mountains, she looked so at ease.

They reached a precipice of flat rock hemmed in by prickly brown shrubbery. Anat bent her head and set down the plastic bag she had been carrying in her mouth, it clinked softly on the hard ground. "Careful not to let anything roll away," Adam said and then shoved the a last biscuit into his mouth whole and collapsed gratefully beside the bag, splaying his legs out in front of him and leaning back on his palms. The sphinx lay down on her other side.

"You shall have to open the bottle for me, as your thumbs served me once at the beginning of our friendship, so they must serve me again."

Adam reached over and pulled the two bottles out, they cast shadows like stained glass, honeyed light dancing on the warm stone. "Aw Anat, do you really think I'm your friend?"

"As close to a friend as a sphinx could have, yes."

Adam glanced at her, then out at the view. The town was tucked away out of sight almost directly below them. The forest seethed like an ocean against the mountains as far as the eye could see. Pillars of light split the scene in shadow, adding its own dimensions. Everything seemed starker, closer, an elegant tapestry. Not a real sunset. The air was warm; since they had arrived Adam hadn't felt a breeze at all. "You never struck me as the solitary sort, to be honest."

"I enjoy talking, I enjoy company. But I am not like you, Adam."

"What's that supposed to mean?"

"You're not meant to be alone." She paused, a small frown creasing her brow. "I do wonder - perhaps I have encountered the occasional solitary human, but I had also forgotten how distant your kind have become from nature. You would not have survived on the island - you never once admitted it, it was me that suggested an alternative. You have barely eaten, perhaps I had less understanding of your kind than I assumed but even I can see your body is damaged and exhausted. You yourself reminded me of pain. You have willingly put yourself through far more than you ever needed to in order to stay here, with me, on this little goose chase of ours. I have come to recognise that in your willingness to follow me, there is a part of you driven to an extreme. I sensed such desperation when we met; I had hoped to soothe it, but each choice you make conflicts with your very nature, you were not meant for this."

Adam laughed, it was his turn to give an oddly forced, jovial tone. "It bloody must've been a while! You've only looked at your drink and you're getting all philosophical." He leaned over and elbowed her gently in the side. She turned her cursed eyes on him. He hated when she stared at him like that. To avoid looking back, he set about opening the bottles, grateful for the bottle opener they had found as he pulled it out of the bag. The beer smelled a little stale, but a cautious sip deemed it at least drinkable. He set Anat's drink beside her large front paw, and took a swig of his own.

Anat heaved herself onto her hind legs, revealing a surprisingly ruffled underbelly. Slowly, carefully, she gripped the bottle between her two padded forelimbs, lifting it carefully to her face in a pose that unexpectedly reminded Adam of a giant squirrel. He bit back a laugh.

"I have grown very fond of you Adam. I am glad I didn't poison you with my breath the other night, I'm glad I chose you for my plan to escape. But you do puzzle me."

Adam watched, fascinated, as she tipped back her head and poured a good half of the content from the bottle into her mouth, revealing for the first time a second row of teeth behind the fangs he had seen, all glinting in the light. He felt his heart squeeze with familiar fear. She really wasn't human. "Puzzle you?" he croaked.

It is as if you are afraid of how you might burden me until you feel you must dig out some secret grudge. It is as if you are so afraid of being left alone, you make yourself alone anyway, which is a contradiction in the most glaringly obvious sense. It is a riddle I have seen many times in humans and I still can't understand; how you could do to yourself the things you fear the most, without even thinking of it so? You need people Adam. Why did you ask for this? Why are you here?"

Adam looked out over the heartbreaking, breathtaking view. He'd been avoiding trying to think too much, ever since he'd met her at the museum. He felt oddly betrayed. Up until now, Anat had been a reason not to think, their adventures had landed him with a bang in the here, the now, the abilities and limits of his body. But even in the confines of his body, he supposed thought had continued to haunt him. His guilt dragged at him every time she looked him in the eye.

"Have I ever told you, have you ever heard of *The Sphinx*?"

Anat's steady eyes were on him once again. Eyes so human and yet so strange. "Of course. I am a sphinx, and I know of the Great Sphinx of Egypt, amongst others, though I prefer not to meet him."

If he had been in another headspace, Adam might have pestered her for more information on this. As it was, he just said, "No! No, not like - it's a poem. By uh... Oscar Wilde. I read it when I was a kid. I'm not into poetry, it was for school. It was about him struggling with his... Well, I'd forgotten about it until the other day, you know. To be honest, I didn't even really like it at the time. Haven't read any poetry since. School, I mean. You reminded me I guess."

He looked down at the battered ruins of his shoes, scuffed the toes at the dust, trying to find the shape of what he was trying to say, trying to fight the twisting serpents of feeling and memory into something she might understand. "I was kind of a funny kid. I got picked on a lot..."

He looked at Anat. Her face hadn't changed. She just stared at him, as still as when he had first laid eyes on her, waiting for him to continue.

"I don't like thinking about stuff. You know? Or nothing hard. I always just shut it down. Any weird thoughts, or weird feelings."

He scrubbed a hand through his hair. "Sometimes I worry I'm forgetting things. I don't know. I guess when you - when we met, I saw an opportunity to lean into it. To just let everything go." He hugged his wandering hands tightly round him, liked the comfort, held himself tighter as he rocked.

"Everyone back home..." He paused, home seemed like the wrong word, but he pressed on, "... everyone back there thinks I'm this stand-up bloke, you know? Always up for a casual gaff, always out for a laugh. I never *talk* to anyone, you know? I don't even know how. I'm doing shit right now. They didn't - They never really tried - I don't think anyone would even miss me. I don't even miss anyone. Over a decade in the same bloody city, and all I miss is a tuna crunch." He gave an attempt at a chuckle, still holding onto himself. "I guess, what I'm trying to say is..."

"I'm scared." His voice cracked embarrassingly. "Being with you felt less alone than anyone else in my life right now, which is stupid because you're a big stone monster and I know bloody nothing about you. But we chat, and you've taken me places I never thought I'd see and - I don't want to be left alone. I don't want to be alone again. I've been not thinking about stuff and lying to myself and it's all just a big tangled mess, and I did it to myself. I don't even know why I'm here..." He trailed off. Nothing he had said was an explanation, if anything he had just added to her question.

Anat's face remained unreadable. She lowered herself into a crouch. "Climb onto my back, I must show you something."

10⊕

*Why are you tarrying? Get hence! I
weary of your sullen ways,
I weary of your steadfast gaze, your somnolent
magnificence.*

They flew through the lilac throes of twilight the dying sun cast round herself. Adam clung tightly to Anat's mane, the wind cooled his cheeks and ran a soothing hand through his hair.

He couldn't tell how long they flew for, but when they landed it was dark. It took him a little while to get his bearings. They were in some kind of field, with scratchy, dry grass. Far in the distance he could hear the strange, familiar thrum of speakers, see coloured lights, dancing shadows. Adam turned to Anat. He could only faintly see her - there was no moon to aid him, and the lights from the town were too far away. "Why did you bring me here?"

"There is a festival over there. They have been having it every year since I was first hewn. I think you would enjoy it, I hear they are welcoming to strangers."

Anat seemed to be getting further way, Adam stepped forward. "Why did you bring me here Anat?"

"Maybe I cannot understand you, or feel the complexities of the despair you feel. But I have seen many a generation of man deny themselves their nature, and cast each other down in the name of false reason. You are a human; to love is in your nature. To deny your nature because it does not fit what you were led to believe you should be is to deny happiness, wherever you are. I know you were not happy where I found you. But this is a new place, a fresh start. You have escaped, you should be proud, your fate is fulfilled. Return to human company Adam."

Adam just shook his head, he kept shaking it. Anat suddenly turned and disappeared into the undergrowth. With a cry, Adam leapt after her, stumbled in the dark to his knees, found to his aggravation he was crying again. "I'm not ready for this! Don't leave! Anat. *Anat!* Don't leave..."

Suddenly she was upon him. For a brief moment, Adam was afraid. Anat pulled at him roughly with her paws, he could feel her skin scraping his cheek, her claws at his back - it took him a moment to realise he had been pulled into a hug. "I am not leaving because I do not like you Adam. I am sorry. I cannot be the friend you want, but this is what you need."

Adam hugged her back. It was ridiculously uncomfortable, but he held on tight for a long time anyway. Eventually, he stepped back, sniffing, and tugging at the hem of his tattered shirt.

"I'm sorry about all this. Genuinely, thank you." He looked up at her, luminous night eyes like twin moons glowing in the dark. "I know I've not been the easiest passenger. It means a lot to me that you cared enough to bring me here." His voice wobbled a bit, but stayed firm. "I'll miss you Anat. I might not have a sphinx's memory, but I'll keep you in mine all the same."

Anat smiled, her teeth suddenly set gleaming. "If you see anything stranger in the world, drop them my name, though I doubt you will. Goodbye, Adam."

He heard the dramatic hiss of her wings, and then she was gone. Adam wiped his face on his sleeve one more time for good measure. He was going to look insane walking into a town like this. He didn't even have any money on him, or an idea of what currency to expect, for that matter. The thought was a little thrilling. He shoved his hands deep in his pockets, took a deep breath, and began to head cautiously towards the moving crush of warm human bodies under the dancing coloured lights.

~

See, the dawn shivers round the grey gilt-dialled
towers, and the rain
Streams down each diamonded pane and blurs
with tears the wannish day.

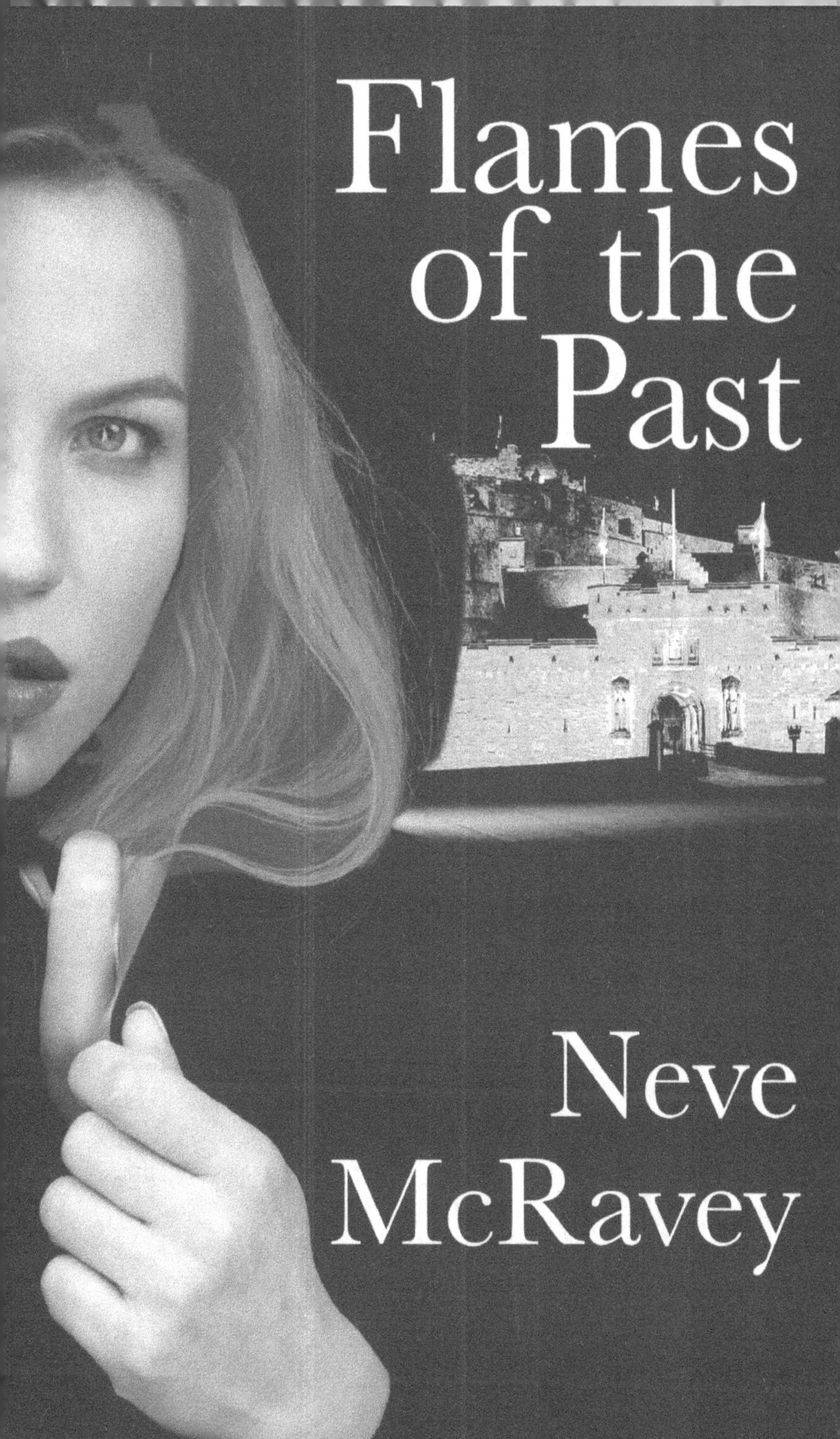

Flames of the Past
Neve McRavey

1

Chris

I never believed in magic until I met her. With a devilish smile and flecks of gold in her green eyes, the girl was bewitching. You could say she cursed me to an endless life of longing for something I will never quite reach, or you could even say I was tangled under her spell. But I believe she opened my mind to the world around us. Whatever hell she may have raised, Isobel Finnie was my taste of heaven.

It was a feverish August night with only the glow of the street-lights tearing through the ebony of Edinburgh's cobble lanes, when I first met magic.

The blurry night dragged on, pouring shots and cleaning glasses. It was a Tuesday night in August and the bar was desolate, apart from a few scattered flushed faces. I was pulled through the evening by a few pints and the thought of returning to my bed. The music played on repeat all night until the noise singed my ears and I shut the system down altogether.

Nights at the bar were usually fun. I got to see everything: drunk friends fighting; questionable dance moves; couples falling in and out of alcohol-induced love. Beneath the faded lights, I began to see people. Through observations, I got to know couples who were lost in each other's eyes, oblivious to the world, or lonely souls who were searching across the crowds to find a friendly face. However, I was never that face.

I, too, felt lonely. The only difference between them and me was that I was protected by a facade when I stood behind the bar. In my own oak wood fort, I laughed and splashed a few drinks while I noticed every detail of every person who attracted my interest. My eyes crept along faces between the cluster, trying to gain a better understanding of each personality. I would scan their eyes – some masked by eyeshadow, others exposed; I found that eyes said a lot about a person.

But tonight, in the bar, I didn't *see* anyone. There was no intriguing ambience surrounding anyone that night, so I found myself drifting into boredom's arms. The job was only to get me through my last few years at university, to which I would be returning to in September. Working late nights were not always ideal for early morning starts at uni, but it paid for my rent, books, and a few drinks at the student union.

I was studying Social Anthropology at the University of Edinburgh, with no plans for the future. I loved learning, absorbing information about the world. Cultures fascinated me, but I felt like I was dragging myself through university. I feared it would be a struggle to survive the two years I had left. I had no job prospects, no ambitions; I was just a little lost.

Despite the long shifts, working at the bar suited me fine. The hours were flexible enough and I was able to balance my workload, a social life, and earning an income. The tips were decent and the atmosphere was fun. I didn't really have much to complain about.

Gary, the boss, let me away a little earlier than usual, however not early enough. A loud sigh escaped my mouth as I wrapped up in my jacket and saw the rain hit the ground like bricks falling from the sky. I stepped out and began to walk home.

My eyes hung heavy as I made my way home from another long shift. The raindrops held onto the leaves above me, begging not to be dropped, but the leaves were not strong enough to hold their might and, like glass, the raindrops shattered on the stone. The trees hung over me as I shuffled hastily home. Tucked away under a hood, I kept my eyes on the ground, trying to dance around the falling pellets as if they would not see and hit me. The bitter air stung my cheeks, and I didn't dare look up to the moon as I knew I would take a swift punch from the wind.

Darkness turned me into nothing but an ominous silhouette, jaunting home. With my red, raw hands that had been bitten by the crisp frost of the air, I tried to adjust my hood to shelter me further. As my hands brushed by my face, a neon red sign sparkled at the corner of my eye.

The sign buzzed, like bees drawing honey. Having crossed this path a hundred times before, I was startled at this new sight. It excited me. Having acquired a sudden impulse for whatever was inside, I walked through their doors.

The rain rolled off of me as I stepped inside and I was instantly hit by the smell of coffee as welcome heat wrapped around me. The soft rock music vibrated from the speakers. The bass of the tune rang in my chest and the female singer's raspy tone instantly made me feel warm.

I stumbled between empty wooden chairs, estranged from their round tables. The shop looked haunted by isolation; not a single soul rested there. Each step echoed as my foot kissed the floor until I found myself distracted by the tall brunette who stood behind the bar. With her back turned to me, subtly nodding her head to the music, her short chocolate hair waved as she danced slightly.

Her hand was in the back pocket of her black denims as she swayed, pouring liquid into a cup. Sweat began to soak my palms as I approached her. As if someone had their hand wrapped around my throat, I couldn't find the words I needed to get her attention. A sudden nervousness consumed me and I questioned what on earth made me feel like this. Maybe it was the heat from the coffee machine.

Lost in thought, I tripped on the leg of a chair, creating a screeching scream as it dragged along the floor. Instantly, with a slight feeling of guilt, I looked at the girl. Startled, she jumped to meet my eyes.

Her stare pierced right through me, a striking green ocean surrounding her wide, black pupils. Her eyes were like vacuums; I was absorbed into her. Little gold flecks were sprinkled in her iris and I saw magic in her eyes. Framed by long eyelashes, a slight flick with eyeliner, her eyes drowned me in the green. She blinked and I snapped out of my daze.

'I'm sorry,' she giggled with a strong accent, rougher than my own. 'I got a fright.'

Blood rushed to my cheeks as she spoke, and heat rushed up my neck. I felt embarrassed, as though I was committing a crime by looking at those eyes. I felt guilty. As if for hundreds of years, I had done her wrong. Yet I tried to mask my humiliation, and laughed.

'It's okay, I'm sorry. I must've given you a fright.' I really was sorry. 'I didn't realise this place was here?' I said the words like a question and she had the explanation to my oblivion.

'Yeah, open twenty-four hours!' With a sarcastic high pitch to her smoky voice and a tired expression pulling at her eyes, she looked down and shook her head, scratching at her skull.

While she spoke, I tried to escape from her eyes. I dragged my gaze down her pale skin to meet her lips that were a little torn but pink with heat, in the shape of a heart. Freckles, like little kisses, dotted across her nose.

She tucked her curls behind her ear and asked, 'What can I get you?'

I didn't actually know how to answer. I wasn't a coffee fanatic; in fact, I didn't believe that drinks should be hot. I thought there was something slightly perverse about it. But how could I have explained the undeniable pull I'd felt to come inside? Interest had gravitated me towards the sign and I couldn't resist. Usually, I was quick on my feet, but there was something about this girl that stifled me.

I swallowed my pride and replied, 'I just never noticed this place. I work at Black Cats up the road.'

She laughed and shook her head as she popped open a Diet Coke and poured it into a tall coffee glass. I raised an eyebrow. 'You don't look like much of a coffee man,' she said.

I chuckled in disbelief. She was able to see right through me. A moment of childish fear came over me, and as I looked into those eyes once more, I could've sworn she knew each and every one of my deepest, darkest secrets. Like Medusa, it was the eyes that made me uneasy. Or maybe it was her eyes that drew me in.

I'm unsure what about me screamed 'not-a-coffee-man', but she had clearly picked up on it straight away. I shook my head, sceptical about how she could read so much into me, but maybe I was being paranoid. Maybe I was just a very non-coffee-like person. But she was right, I fucking hated coffee.

Change jingled as I reached into my pocket for money and stretched my neck up, as though the ceiling would direct my hands where to find a few pound coins. With a sense of urgency, she blurted out, 'Don't be daft. It's on me.'

A kind gesture from a stranger. You could see she was kind; she had kind eyes, the type that always seemed as though they were smiling. She was pretty, too. Her smile looked almost too large for her face, with sparkling teeth and deep dimples. There was a quiet attractiveness about her.

I thanked her, but didn't return to a seat or leave. I couldn't drag myself away. Instead, I stayed standing at the desk. Bending on her knees, her eyes crawled up to meet mine. She smiled.

With a chuckle, she asked, 'Staying?'

I shook my head, realising I was still staring at her, frozen in the same spot. However, I couldn't bring myself to leave. 'If that's okay with you.' I smirked.

Her head shook and she laughed to herself. I think the offer of my company came as a surprise. Her eyes pierced through mine as she untied her apron. 'Fine by me. I'll join you.'

My heart began to flutter as she spoke. Her looks were enchanting. She wasn't necessarily striking, but with each glance, her beauty became more apparent. My eyes were glued to her; it was an effort to tear my gaze away. Her face was perfectly unsymmetrical; not like a model, more like art. Far from a blank canvas, every glance revealed something new; another freckle, different colours in her eyes. She really was art.

Stuck in a gaze, I had to snap myself out of the dream I was in. She raised an eyebrow as she joined me at the round table, a large ceramic mug snuggled between her hands. The chains on her boots jingled as she approached where I sat with a smile painted on her face and narrow eyes.

'Isobel Finnie.' Introducing herself with an awkward confidence, she took one hand from her mug to reach mine, before she sat down. Isobel Finnie. I took her hand in mine and shook.

'Nice to meet you, Isobel Finnie. I'm Chris.' Holding my eyes, she smiled. There was a nervous tension between us both, but she seemed to erase it with her cool ease.

'Christopher McCarthy,' I added.

She sat down, now content with the knowledge I had just provided. Her green eyes pierced through me but she refused to break eye contact. Before any silence formed between us, she cut through it.

'So, who are you?'

I laughed and pulled my gaze from hers, only to look back up and find her eyes biting through mine. Her lack of words suggested she was still expecting an answer from me.

Shrugging my shoulders, I racked my brain for anything interesting, but failed. 'I'm twenty. I'm in my second year at uni—'

She cut me off before I could finish. 'What uni are you at?'

'Edinburgh.'

Her eyes lit up as I spoke. She couldn't conceal the smile appearing on her face. 'No way! I'm starting in September. What are you studying?'

I giggled with excitement. Butterflies started to flap in my stomach for a reason which was unclear to me. 'Social anthropology. You?'

'Scottish literature and Scottish history. I don't know anyone; I've only just moved here.' I knew her accent was a little different from mine; I guessed at Glasgow. 'I'm from Paisley.'

She continued to sip at the coffee, snuggled between her hands, in front of her face. The steam danced into the air from her cup, creating a little cloud of mist in front of her eyes.

'I take it you've heard about Helen Gowdie?'

Edinburgh was haunted by the news of Helen Gowdie. It was the talk of the town; a tragedy on everyone's lips.

Isobel nodded her head before standing up to make her way over to the counter and lifting a newspaper. She let it fall from her hand onto the table. I had seen the same heading on every other newspaper and plastered over social media, yet it didn't fail to strike me hard.

GIRL, 19, MURDERED

Helen Gowdie, a 19-year-old student studying at the University Of Edinburgh, has been found dead. According to the post-mortem, Gowdie was brutally beaten before being drowned and her body burned. Gowdie is the latest victim in what appears to be a series of similar murders.

I dragged my eyes from the paper. I knew the rest. No suspects. No motive. Only an innocent young woman's life taken. The rumour mill was constantly spinning with the gossip.

'Yeah, oh my god, it's so terrible. So sad,' I said softly.

She looked down and stirred her coffee with her finger before sticking it in her mouth. With her finger still between her lips, she spoke. 'I saw the pictures, too.'

'Yeah, I heard there were photos posted online. I tried my best to avoid them.' I'd failed, though. It was impossible to not see her body. Or at least, what was left of it. 'The comments left on the photos were worse than the pictures themselves, eh?'

'Why did everyone hate her so much?' Isobel's voice broke a little with hurt, as if it was she who had received those comments.

'I don't really know,' I lied. I had seen the comments calling the girl a slut, slag, too loud, annoying. She had a style that was a little out-there. People called her a Satanist and a goth. She unsettled them. I knew why people didn't like her.

'It's like a witch hunt,' she said casually, as if she had heard it one hundred times.

She sounded so unfazed by what she had just said, I wondered if it was an attempt at a joke I had misinterpreted. My mouth must have dropped, or I must have subconsciously raised an eyebrow, because she seemed shocked by the reaction that I tried to conceal. She sounded so unfazed by what she had just said, I wondered if it was an attempt at a joke I had misinterpreted.

'She was murdered in the same way women accused of witchcraft were. Hundreds, if not thousands, of people happy that she's gone. It isn't a reach to say it's like a witch hunt.' She laughed.

I chuckled and shook my head; it just sounded so ridiculous. However, Isobel seemed to have intelligence follow her. A charisma that made you want to believe each and every word she spoke. She had a charm, supported by wisdom. Because the words came from her mouth, I allowed myself to question the possibility of it all.

'I think people felt threatened by a woman who was a little different. People can't trust what they don't know. Some women can't be contained, so they are murdered.' She spoke with no hint of anger within her voice, as though she was simply stating facts. Which I suppose, she was.

A little lost for words, I looked down and picked at my nails.

My head lifted as Isobel hesitantly asked, 'Did you know her?'

Helen was the same age as me and at the same university. I must have crossed her path a few times, being on similar courses, in and out of the same buildings. But I didn't recognise her face when it was shown on the news, nor in the pictures people had laid by the memorial at the uni.

Embarrassed, I shook my head and a delicate quiet arose between us. We let it lie there for a few minutes before I asked, 'So, are you into all that?'

With a chuckle, she met my eyes, her own sparkling with warmth. 'Feminism? Yeah, I would say I'm into basic human rights.' She was witty and fast, jumping back at me.

'I mean, you just seemed to know about witchy stuff.'

She paused, as if processing what I had just said. A little hurt glistened in her eyes and she opened her mouth to speak, but no words came out. She stopped herself from saying anything. I worried I had upset her; said something I wasn't supposed to. But she just smiled and took my empty can from me and took her own mug back behind the bar. It was my cue to leave.

I began to gather myself together and stood up, only to be turned around by her voice.

'Chris?'

'Yeah?'

'Come by again.' She smiled warmly at me and I smiled back, ensuring her that I definitely would.

When I got home, I submerged myself underneath my bedcovers and let sleep take hold of me. She blessed my dreams that night, not leaving my imagination. I didn't want to wake up.

2

Isobel

I lay in, with my eyes open, frightened to sleep because I knew what dreams awaited me. Since moving to Edinburgh, the same nightmares kept me awake. Dreams of women drowning in freezing cold waters haunt my sleep. Icy waves suffocating their lungs, burying them underneath the bleak seas. They gasp for air, only to be impaled with the biting waters, pushing them further down into the deep blackness.

Some miraculously survive. But not for long. Dragged from the water, drenched in the raw bitterness of the cold, begging for their lives, the women plead with the cheering crowds. Men tower over their frail bodies, thrusting them against a wooden stake. The mob cheer for their blood as the women sob. Fully aware of their forthcoming, some accept their fate and begin to curse those who have sentenced them to an early demise. Others pray, imploring their survival. However, there is no potential for their lives; the mob have already convicted each woman before her trial.

I had grown up with the knowledge that I was a descendant of Agnes Finnie; it was something our family wouldn't have allowed me to forget. 'Remember what they did to her,' was the response when I would slightly complain. Agnes Finnie had been accused of witchcraft in the 17th century, then hanged and burnt at the stake. She'd suffered the same fate as thousands of women of her time. Independent women, widows, sexual beings – all labelled as witches. They had danced with the devil, so – inevitably – had to be terminated. We didn't learn about any of this in history classes. And, growing up, I doubted that my family was telling me the truth about our ancestors. It wasn't until I reached my teenage years that I began to branch out. Once I researched the witch trials, I was hooked. A fire was lit within my chest and I refused to let go of the anger. I couldn't fathom how women had been murdered for being women.

My granny would always laugh at me and say, 'If they said your great-great-great-great-great-great-great grandmother was a witch, she had nothing on you.' That fire in my stomach often got me into trouble. I inherited my mother's rage, and I think that the fire burned a little too hot for most people. I wanted to leave that behind and have a fresh start in Edinburgh.

I had moved to escape the reputation that had been branded upon me. The flaming rumours were difficult not to suffocate beneath, and I hoped Edinburgh would bring me a new life. But I was beginning to fear that Edinburgh was playing with my head.

Knowing that someone that I shared the same blood with had been murdered in these streets, must have had some affect on my mental state. Well, it was clearly manipulating my dreams.

A pang of guilt struck me as I realised my roommate must have heard me screaming while I slept. The walls in our little flat were as thin as paper; I was hesitant to lean anything against them in fear of them collapsing. Sometimes I woke myself up from my dreams with my screams; there was no way in the world that she could peacefully ignore them.

Usually, I would be mortified, but I allowed myself to fall into Dallas's trust. She had become an almost big sister figure to me since I had moved here. She was only the year above me, but her experience largely outweighed my lack of. I didn't like the idea of needing to be looked after, but I had quickly accepted her guidance, realising the real world was much scarier than in the movies. She had taught me more in the few weeks of living with her than I had known in my whole life back in Paisley.

Dallas was like a real-life Barbie doll. She was the type of girl you instantly admire, as everything she does seems so graceful. We were an unlikely pairing, but we adored living with each other, and our friendship had quickly blossomed into a sisterhood. She was a proper girl.

I had never really had a girl friend before Dallas; I was the kind of powerhouse that girls don't usually like. Walking into every room, I would be shot with looks as deadly as bullets and knew every muttered conversation revolved around how I much of a 'bitch' I was.

It was ironic, because I believed that it was us girls against the world. I had been brought up in a household where I was told that girls were to look out for each other and that men were the ones to be feared. But instead, we were pitted against each other. And knowing that my own sisters couldn't protect me, I lost trust in almost everyone.

Because of that, living with Dallas was a breath of fresh air.

As much as it broke my heart to leave home, we all knew that I couldn't stay there any longer without having people roll their eyes each time they heard my name. I needed out of that town. I couldn't have coped much longer with knowing I was the most hated girl there.

I wondered if Helen Gowdie had felt the same way.

My heart broke for her. I pictured her curled up into a little ball on her bed, in the early hours of the morning. I heard her cry herself to sleep. I felt her heart break, and I knew what it was like. Even in death, Helen was still receiving the hate she had in life. I wish I had known her. I wish I could have given her a cuddle and told her it would be okay. I wish I could have been a friend.

I thought of earlier that night and how friendly Chris was to me. I hoped he was the first of many and that the comments on Helen's post didn't reflect the majority of the people I would meet here. I just wanted to make a few friends.

3

Chris

The streetlights replaced the stars in the night sky as we made our way through town. After a hard week of working, Cameron had begged me to have a night out with him, so I'd agreed.

The air was hot. Girls and boys flocked like animals, thirsty, to a watering hole. The night air was riddled with the stench of alcohol, sweat, and desperation. Each and every single one of us was looking for a kill tonight; to catch our prey.

However, that prey came in different forms. Some of us only wanted a night out, an escape from the reality that consumed us. Others wanted someone to keep them company for the rest of the summer's night. Some wanted a few laughs with friends, to get pissed and fall about, to make memories. I don't know what I wanted. A little taste of everything, I suppose.

As we made our way into the queue, Cameron turned away from me with delight on his face. I followed his gaze to see three girls walking towards us. He stepped out of the line; I stayed in my place. He put his arm around one of the three – a pretty girl with long legs and blonde waves falling over her shoulders. She strutted towards the club, Cameron still wrapped around her.

As they approached me, Cameron explained, 'Chris, this is Dallas. She's on my course.'

Dallas. I liked that name; I hadn't ever met anyone with it. We exchanged smiles as her friends caught up with her. A shorter girl with bright eyes and an alcohol-induced cheerful grin began to introduce herself as Fiona. She leaned in, confidently, for an introductory hug. I awkwardly allowed myself to hug her back until a voice interrupted.

'No way! Hello, stranger!' I knew the voice instantly. The deep, coarse Glaswegian accent was instantly recognisable. How could I ever forget? My eyes were met by Isobel's. She smiled; her bright teeth framed by fire-red lips. A heavenly glow surrounded her, created by the warm streetlight above. She wore a red satin dress, and her wild curls fell freely over her shoulders.

'Hello,' I replied, trying to conceal my excitement. And without any more words, just an affectionate gaze between us, we made our way into the club.

As we headed down the stairs into the darkness of the basement , my eyes were fixed on her hips, swaying side to side in red satin, dancing as she shuffled in her heeled boots.

Noticing this, Cameron struck me with his elbow. As I cried out, he glared disapprovingly at me. 'Don't think about it,' he hissed in my ear.

'What?' I scrunched my face up at him.

'She's a pure slag, mate. I heard from Jamie that she had to move here from Glasgow 'cause she'd shagged every guy there.'

'Fuck off, Cammy!' I barked at him.

As Isobel looked over her shoulder, I noticed how her eyes glowed and, somehow, looked apologetic. I wondered if what

Cameron said was true, and whether it would matter. I decided not to worry about her reputation tonight.

The night began to turn into a blur, drawing by us. At the start, we kept our distance from the girls, but it wasn't long before Isobel and I were exchanging flirty glances with one another. She threw her hands above her head and laughed with her friends, the brightly coloured lights bouncing off her, lighting her up like a rainbow. Even in the darkness, she remained a glowing ray of light.

Isobel and I were naturally drawn to each other. Caught in an intoxicated haze, we couldn't seem to let go of each other's gaze. We gravitated towards each other like magnets, unable to be pulled away. With a sudden boost of confidence that the vodka gave me, I placed my hand on her hip. As we touched, my fingertips began to tingle. Electricity.

Only communicating through our eyes, we moved together as we danced. We just clicked. Over the music, I shouted into her ear, 'Do you smoke?'

She shook her head, but instead of anticipating my response, she placed her hand on my shoulder and replied in my ear, 'No, but I'll come outside with you for one.'

She took my hand and led me up the stairs, out of the club. Her hands remained cold, despite my clammy palms. Her gold rings stacked on her finger tickled my skin and the bracelets bounced off her wrists to hit mine with a pretty jingle.

The music was still vibrating through our bodies, beating against our chests, as we left. A smile came across my face; I tried to fight it but couldn't. The girl was absolutely striking. Her face glowed, her eyes sparkled. We fled the heat from the club and ran into the drizzling night. Little raindrops glistened in her dark hair, like tiny pieces of broken glass.

We stumbled out of the bar, giggling for no reason apart from the intoxication we shared, saying stupid things that just triggered the other into a fit of hysterics. The cold air bit at our skin and I pitied her in that little dress. The freezing air broke bumps from my skin but I didn't care.

I lit a cigarette and placed it between my lips. 'Want to get out of here?' I asked, between puffs. Isobel took the cigarette from my mouth and inhaled, nodding her head.

She lifted her phone to her ear and tried to phone us a taxi. To hers, to mine, to a McDonald's… I didn't care. Excitement made my heart skip a few beats, or maybe it was just the vodka Red Bulls. But I was willing to go anywhere with her. I would've stood all night in the cold with her, until the sun tore through the ground into a blood red sky.

She began to gently shiver, her legs shaking like leaves in the autumn. The wind of the night was a gentle reminder of our home country – it might only be autumn, but winter is never far away in Scotland.

She put the phone down and told me that we'd need to wait an hour-and-a-half for a taxi. The thought of us spending more time together tightened my chest with excitement.

'Let's get food!' she exclaimed with a smile on her face, as she wrapped her hand around mine.

I didn't want her to let go. Her words began to blur as she continued to speak, and I found myself becoming more and more lost in her. Absolutely infatuated with her.

'Isobel?' I interrupted her as she began to pull me away to start walking.

She looked from the ground and met my eyes with a sparkle. As if under a spell, a force that I could not fight drew me closer towards her. I edged my feet closer to her body and freed my hand from her grasp to touch her face. I needed to be close to her. She looked up into my eyes and smiled, as if she knew exactly what she was doing. Nervously, I chuckled and so did she.

Every hair on my body shot up as she placed her hand on top of mine on her neck. I stuttered as I spoke, through both nerves and the cold. 'C-can I kiss you?'

I was terrified I had stepped out of line, but I couldn't not ask. I couldn't stop the overwhelming feeling that I needed to kiss her.

'Yeah, Chris.' She replied gently with a giddy smile on her face. 'You can kiss me.'

She leaned into me, soothing her hands around my neck as I pulled her waist closer into my body and grabbed the back of her neck. I kissed her hard, leaving no room to breathe. She kissed me back harder.

Grabbing at each other, we smiled as we kissed, laughing as our lips left each other. Eventually, we pulled away from each other and smiled; a funny kind of grin. The kind that says we both know this is only the beginning and, God, was I excited for the rest of our story.

4

Isobel

I was dragged from my deep slumber by a pounding head-ache and an unbearable dryness stuck to my throat. I couldn't help but let out a groan as I rolled over to get out of bed. The room spun around me as I tried to focus my eyes on anything they would allow me. My coffee curls had fallen from their form and developed into frizz overnight. A familiar feeling of filth clung to my hair and my skin; I was in desperate need of a shower. I stank of hangover. Memories from the night before struck my mind with the great force of embarrassment. In the simplest of terms, I had the fear.

Dallas's awkward footsteps, pattering on the wooden floors outside my door, indicated that she was up and ready for a chat about last night's antics. I laughed at her shadow peeking through the crack of light underneath my door. She didn't want to disturb me, but she was desperate to spill her gossip. I had to mentally prepare myself to break from the cuddles that my bed duvet was supplying me with. Enclosed by the white wonders of the comfort of my bed, I refused to leave just yet.

'Dallas! You up?' I moaned, knowing she definitely was.

She burst through the door, bouncing in her pink pyjama set. Like a blinding bright light, Dallas's entrance forced me to pull my duvet over my head. She yanked the duvet to reveal my face, tarnished with the remainder of last night's make-up. Her perfect blonde curls were neatly tucked into a ponytail, still intact from the previous evening. She threw herself into my bed beside me, pushing me over. Her high energy was a little too much for me so early in the morning.

'So, what's the gossip?' she asked, turning on her side to face me.

I shook my head. 'Nothing really, we—'

Before I even had the chance to finish, Dallas asked what she was dying to know. The real question that was bothering her. 'Did you sleep with him?'

'No!' I shrieked. Dallas chuckled accusingly. 'Honestly, nothing happened. He walked me home.'

'You walked home? Was that not quite a trek?'

'Aye. I mean, it didn't feel too bad. It must've been the drink.'

'Did you see the fire, then?'

'Fire?' I questioned.

'Oh my god, haven't you heard?' Dallas's voice trembled a little.

'What happened?'

'St Giles' Cathedral went up in flames.'

My jaw dropped. I pictured the iconic building crumbling down. The dreadful image of the gothic architecture being torn through by wicked flames, the smoke filling the air. The town's population gathering round to see their prized possession burn like the flames of hell. A fire that would allow no negotiations for goodwill. The heat tearing ruthlessly through the church. The crackling of the wood hissing in the people's ears, whispering. The blaze heightening the church, despite devouring it. The heat burning on people's faces but nothing compared to the tears burning in their eyes. All that was left to do was watch the merciless flame take their treasure, the church.

I could've cried then. Without having any deep connection to the church, I still felt like my heart had been ripped from my chest. One of the most iconic, gorgeous buildings in the city I was beginning to fall in love with had been destroyed. It was soul-destroying.

The memory of walking home past the church pounded in my head. Stumbling in a drunk haze, I remember falling into Chris and holding his eyes in mine, hoping to find adventure in them. As I collapsed into him, I hoped I would never have to fall again. We kissed in front of the church, underneath the starlit skies and surrounded by buildings that had stories hidden in their bricks. I fell in love with the city as I fell for him. I wondered if maybe we had known each other in a past life because, from the first moment we had met, he felt like home.

We giggled like schoolchildren as he reached for his phone and took a selfie. He pressed his lips against my cheek, and I smiled. Not the kind of smile you smile when you know that there is a photo being taken; a real one, full of happiness that you can't fake.

The church, at that moment, was intact. The stars dimly lit the colours in the stained-glass windows and the bricks of the church glowed with the moonlight. The building towered over us with all its might. Beautiful yet so overpowering. The size of it could be intimidating, yet it seemed so gracious.

Suddenly, it came rushing back to me. Blurry memories, as if someone had put film over my eyes. I remembered a few men, dressed in black, staggering around the church. They had almost blended into the darkness of the night, except that one of them held a match. The little spark illuminated his face with a harsh yellow glow.

'What are they doing, Chris?' I remembered asking, sobering up a little.

Chris grabbed my arm and hurried me along. 'Come on, Isobel.'

I pulled my arm from his grip and turned to the men. 'Hey!' I shouted.

They looked our way and shrugged, before turning back to each other.

'Hey!' I shouted again, a little more aggressively this time.

'What is it?' one of them shouted back at me in a husky deep voice. His voice bellowed through the air towards me.

'What are you doing?' I asked.

'Tell your burd to mind her own business,' another one shouted, directed at Chris.

'I'm not his *burd*. What are you doing?'

Chris pulled me by my waist towards him as one of the men came marching towards us. He towered over me, hovering his face above mine, trying to make me feel small. I looked defiantly up at him. He had a deep cut down the side of his cheek and his skin was rough with stories that I didn't want to know.

'You know,' he came closer so I could feel his breath against my skin, 'you shouldn't go sticking your nose where you don't belong. Don't want to make a name for yourself, eh, babe?'

'I want to know what you're doing playing with matches in the early hours of the morning, dancing around a church.'

'You don't want to know, sweetheart. I promise you that. Now, fuck off.' He spat as he spoke.

I stood defiantly, looking up at him until Chris grabbed my hand and tugged me. 'Come on, Isobel. Let's go.'

'Yeah, *Isobel*, go.' The way the man hissed my name made my stomach twist.

I was angry at Chris for making me leave, but I knew he was only trying to look after us. As we walked away, I knew I couldn't let it go unseen. I tried, as discreetly as possible, to snap a picture of them as we walked away.

'Shit. I took a picture of these guys hanging about outside the church. Could you pass me my phone?' I asked Dallas as I wiped the sleep from my eyes. She reached over and passed me the cracked screen.

As I pressed the button on my phone down to switch it on, my screen was set alight with accusations. Without even entering my password, I was able to scroll through snippets of what was being said about me: *Scum. Hope she gets what she deserves.* My face fell absent as my heart rate began to speed up. I let out a shaky breath and carried on reading. *Where she goes chaos follows.*

Before I even allowed myself to start to shake or hyperventilate with the panic of history repeating itself, I reminded myself that I had done nothing wrong and no matter what anyone could say, I was a strong girl with a strong heart and a strong mind. No matter what I was being accused of this time, I knew that I had a fire for a heart and a kind soul. I was not a bad person.

Dallas looked over my shoulder and a gasp escaped from between her lips. 'Oh, Isobel.'

'It's okay.' I smiled, trying to convince myself. 'I'm okay.'

I entered my password with a little angry sort-of confidence that reassured me *I will be okay*. My throat began to tighten as I opened my phone and was met with words that seemed to stab through me like knives. Each insult pierced into my heart. I clicked on where most of the comments were coming from and realised a page had been created about me. *Burn the bitch.*

As I scrolled down it, I realised that I had been accused of setting the fire. Most of what was being said was coming from familiar faces, scattered names I recognised from my hometown. Girls I had once considered friends at high school. A sharp pang of betrayal hit my chest until I realised that these people had never been my friends. They were the first to turn their backs on me. They would be the first to throw the match. They never owed me so much as respect.

Pictures of the fire at St Giles' were plastered over this page's feed followed by a picture of me. And Chris. His arm was around my shoulder. As we looked into the front lens of his phone camera, his lips against my cheek and with bloodshot eyes, I smiled. In the background, there was St Giles', standing as tall as a mountain.

Is it really a coincidence that Isobel Finnie and her latest victim (tagged: Christopher McCarthy) uploaded a selfie outside St Giles', less than 30 minutes before it caught fire? This girl is a danger to everyone around her and wreaks havoc wherever she goes. Thank God she has left.

'Isobel?'

I inhaled deeply and closed my eyes, begging the tears to stay put. I wished the world would slow down for minute to give me time to work out how I was going to handle this situation.

'Please look at me, Isobel.'

I opened my eyes and swallowed down the lump in my throat. 'I'm fine. It's fine.'

'Isobel, I –' I didn't give Dallas the chance to finish what she was going to say, for fear that in would just burst out crying.

'These are the people I have left behind; they don't matter.' I was lying to both her and myself.

It was as if a dark cloud had hovered over my head and started to pour on my perfect fantasy of starting a fresh life in a new city. My chest hurt with the pain my heart was struggling to take. These people did not know me well enough to judge, but that's what hurt the most. I felt like I couldn't defend myself; they had made up their minds about me and there was no chance I could change their minds. Anything I could do would add fuel to their fires.

In a desperate attempt to defend myself, I posted the picture I had taken of the men that night onto the page. I typed the caption rapidly, desperate to reveal the truth. *I am not the guilty one.*

But instantly, the picture was flooded with negative comments. Their minds were made up; guilty until proven innocent. The crowds were thirsty for blood and had already decided on me as their target. Nothing I could say or do was going to change that.

As Dallas opened her mouth to speak, my phone interrupted her thought with a loud ring.

'Don't even pick it up,' Dallas warned with alarm watering in her eyes.

It was an unknown number, but my despair quickly turned to rage and I was desperate to give someone a piece of my mind. I put the phone to my ear, and instantly the anger diminished and I let out a sigh. I revelled in the relief, as if I had stepped into a warm bath that soothed any dirt from me.

'Isobel? It's Chris.'

I smiled, holding my hand to my face to lean on. 'Hi Chris.' I whispered.

'I'm sorry for posting that photo. I obviously didn't know this would happen. I–'

'No worries, Chris.'

'Fancy a chat over breakfast or something?'

A sigh of relief escaped my mouth and a sense of calm overcame me. Some sort of protection. 'I'd love to.'

5

Chris

My leg bounced underneath the table as I waited for Isobel to come in. I was drowning in guilt, feeling responsible for the online backlash she was facing because of a photo I had posted. People were being so cruel to her, but it had made me question why? What had Isobel done that was so terrible that these people were driven to hate someone with such passion?

I woke up to being tagged on Facebook, underneath a status written by the local police:

Update on St Giles' Fire: Police investigating the fire that destroyed St Giles' are looking for witnesses to provide them with more information. If you were in the area between the hours of 2-5am or have any information, please contact the police.

My friends, having seen the picture of Isobel and me that was taken in front of the church and uploaded at 3am, must have assumed that we saw something and had started to tag me underneath it. I guessed that someone who didn't exactly like

Isobel then put two and two together to know that we had been there. My profile was public; it wouldn't have been difficult.

Yet, I couldn't see an ounce of corruption within Isobel. I couldn't fathom a reason why someone would want to put all the blame on her. Not just someone; it felt like everyone wanted to rally against her. Underneath the black eyeliner, Isobel had these wide innocent eyes that you could not help but get lost in. Strip away the black combat boots, the dark clothes and the chains, and Isobel was nothing more than a cute, loveable girl. She had dewy eyes like cherries, sweet and wide. The kind of innocence every boy wants to corrupt.

The little bell ringing on the door of the coffee shop interrupted my train of thought. Isobel wandered in, scanning the room for my face. She wore black jeans and an oversized checked button-up shirt, unintentionally falling off of her shoulder, revealing a little bit of her collarbone. I smiled and raised my hand as she caught my eyes and laughed, skipping over to where I sat. She had her hair thrown into a messy bun that sat on top her head, with little stray stands escaping the bobble. Her hair was so dark that I could almost see a red shimmer through it.

As she took a seat, she threw her little black rucksack on the chair beside her and clasped her hands on the table. I noticed her eyeliner was missing, and realised how big her eyes really were. On closer inspection, I could see that Isobel didn't have any make-up on at all. A few little spots broke from her skin, and the area underneath her eyes was darker than I had seen before. Yet, Isobel looked fresh-faced, with a glow surrounding her. And her smile was still as striking as ever.

'This is madness, isn't it?' To be a hungover morning, Isobel seemed energetic and a little unfazed by all that was going on. Maybe she hadn't seen what I had. But then again, how couldn't she have? Her name was almost trending on Twitter and we were both being tagged into all sorts of abuse. The whole situation did not allow it to be ignored. It was everywhere you could go; inescapable.

'Yeah, it's mad.'

'Listen, I'm sorry about what they're saying about you.'

She reached for my hand and gently stroked it with her thumb, looking down, as if ashamed.

'Hey,' I said softly, prompting her to look up at me. 'It's not your fault.'

'I didn't want this to happen, Chris. I don't even know half of these people. It's like an angry mob against me' She began to rant, as if needing to defend herself to me.

I wanted to let her know that she didn't need to defend herself to me, that I didn't believe what they were saying about her. And even if I did, I wanted to fix it.

'No, I get it Isobel. Don't worry.'

Isobel's phone started to buzz. She pretended to ignore it for the first few rings, but after a minute, she asked, 'Sorry, do you mind?'

I shook my head as she scrambled through her bag for her phone, pulling out a little black notebook with doodles of stars and moons and flowers scribbled all over.

'Hello?' she answered.

As she spoke, I took the notebook in my hands and glanced at Isobel, as if asking permission to look. She nodded her head swiftly and carried on with her conversation. I flicked through the pages, catching glimpses of words. Surrounded by doodles of bees and flowers, I found a poem:

> *Take your knife and drag it along my skin*
> *To see the wounds weep honey, bleeding thin.*
> *A colony lives within me and chaos thrives,*
> *As there is no queen to rule over the hives.*

Each bee plays a programme part
For I have an anarchic hive in place of my heart.

Isobel chatted away to whoever was on the phone. I assumed it was her friend Dallas, judging by the girl chat. I followed each word with my finger as I read her poem, then flipped to the next page to read the next one. And the next. They were all really good. Isobel hung up the phone and apologised.

'They are all about nature?' I was curious about her poetry.

'What?'

'Your poems.'

'Aw,' she chuckled. 'I guess I've always had a strong connection to nature.'

'That's a nice way to be,'

'Nature takes care of us.'

'Or destroys us,' I debated, smirking at her.

'Tomato, tomato.' She giggled.

'I didn't know you wrote.'

'Yeah, a little bit.'

'I don't know much about poetry, but I can tell they're good.'

'Thanks,' she giggled, tucking her hair behind her ear.

'What was Dallas saying?' I asked.

'Someone's egged the flat window.' She shrugged her shoulders and laughed it off, as if it didn't bother her. I raised my eyebrows in shock. I couldn't believe someone, at our age, had gone out of their way to do something so childish. 'It's not a big deal.'

'That's so bad.' I didn't really know what to say. I wasn't sure she needed consoling.

'It doesn't matter.' The conversation fell silent for a minute as she twirled her finger around her coffee before sticking it in her mouth. 'Want to come back to mine? Dallas is meeting her friends from school. It would be nice to have someone to help clean up the egg. We could maybe go by the police station on our way there?'

'Yeah, of course.'

6

Isobel

As we approached my flat, we noticed something unusual from afar. My front door had been vandalised. In blood red, the word 'Witch' was painted over my door.

Keeping my head above water was a constant struggle. Seeing that online page and reading the constant hate, the looks, the sneers, the insults, the giggles, had became too much to bear. I had been plunged into a constant state of darkness that I did not know how to escape from.

I felt as though I was suffocating underneath the humiliation of it all, but I laughed as I stuck the key in the door and shook my head. Chris didn't look angry or upset. Only hurt. As if *he* had been the one who had come home to find *his* door vandalised with an insult like that. I just didn't want to cry in front of him.

I laughed, shaking my head. I touched my door and saw the paint drip down my fingers, like blood. 'Wow,' I muttered shakily. I didn't allow to say myself to say any more for fear of breaking down.

'Isobel, are you okay?' Chris asked from behind me.

I didn't have the strength to face him.

'I'm fine!' I lied, laughing to conceal my voice breaking. I didn't want him to view me as a victim. I wasn't a victim; I was strong. I had faced a lot worse.

I wanted to allow myself to cry and be sad. I wanted to be alone. I didn't want him to see me like this. I was embarrassed at the tears that started to well in my eyes, like hot coals I wanted rid of. I didn't want him to notice.

Here I am. A girl you barely know, with bags under her eyes that are just as heavy as the baggage it looks as if she comes with. The world hates her so why don't you, Chris? Why are you still here?

I wanted to collapse into him. My heart ached for him to open his arms and allow me to fall into them. I needed comfort. I wanted his arms to wrap around me and him to promise me everything was okay and that he would take care of it. Or Dallas would take care of it. Or anyone... Just not me.

Trying to fiddle my keys into the lock, I said softly, 'I'll just clean this up myself, don't worry. Thanks, Chris.'

I couldn't have gotten away any faster from him. I wanted the ground to swallow me up whole, until I felt his hand place on my shoulder. His touch made every hair on my body rise and my skin began to tingle underneath his hand. He spun me around to look at him, but I couldn't bring myself to meet his eyes; I feared it would break me.

With my gaze glued to my twiddling thumbs, chipping away at my black nail polish, Chris lifted my chin up, between this thumb and index finger, forcing me to meet his eyes. 'We'll take care of this, Isobel.'

The reassurance prompted me to lean on my toes until I could almost reach his face. I ran my thumb gently over his bushy brows that arched so elegantly above his ocean blue eyes. His dirty blond hair fell effortlessly over his forehead. He was so beautiful. He was the distraction I so desperately needed.

'Kiss me, Chris.'

He rested his hands on my waist and pulled me towards his body until the space between us no longer existed. My lips caught his in a hard kiss, and every pounding thought in my head melted as he pulled me closer. He took my face in his hands and the world around us began to fade away.

I slid my hand underneath his leather jacket as his fingers drifted up the back of my shirt. As his skin touched my back, my body was set alight. With a fistful of his hair in one hand and my other hand squeezing his white top, I pulled him deeper into me.

He pressed me against the door, his hand above me dipped into the red paint. I felt the wet paint stick to my back as I moaned into his mouth.

We barely knew each other but I felt as if I was already his. I had never needed someone more than in that moment. It felt so right to have him so close to me. I didn't want him to go.

'Chris,' I breathed, stopping him. I had to fight with myself to get him to stop because I didn't want it to end, but I didn't want him to think I was a slut. If he didn't already.

'I know,' he said, dragging his hand down my face. He pulled back and began to laugh as he looked down at the hand he'd just touched me with. His fingers were totally red, soaked with the paint, and he had just dragged it across my face.

As we both stepped back, I could see we had smudged the paint so much that it looked as if the door was supposed to be that colour.

'I like it,' Chris chuckled.

I decided then and there what I would do next. I knew how I would overcome this. I had already been chased out of one town, and I refused to let go of a city I had already fallen in love with. They weren't going to win this time.

I turned to Chris and asked 'Where can we get more red paint?'

7

Chris

It had been a month since the fire at St Giles'. Walking by nothing but ashes in the city centre must have chipped away at my soul each time I had seen it. Growing up in Edinburgh, I had seen St Giles' as the heart of the city. Somewhere that could always be relied upon. Now it was gone.

But nonetheless, that fire had sparked something else; my relationship with Isobel. In the weeks before university started back up, the days began to fade into each other. We watched the sun travel across the sky each day, yet didn't know when the day started or ended; we were too busy being with each other.

To get to Isobel's flat, I had to pass the ashes of the church. As I did so, I thanked it. The destruction of something so beautiful had resulted in the creation of another. As I thought about it, my heart began to do somersaults, prompting me to start running towards her. To be apart any longer would be painful.

The hate Isobel received online continued. It came in waves, but I never once saw her shed a single tear. If anything, it made her skin tougher and her mind stronger. She barely reacted. I didn't know how she coped with any of it. The bullets that they shot at her were toxic, enough to pierce through anyone. But not Isobel.

I watched our breathing fall into sync as we sat in a comfortable silence. I sat on her bed as she lay her head on my chest. Running my hands through her hair as she wrote, I read my book. From the corner of my eye, I peeked at her notebook to see if I could catch a glimpse of her poetry.

'Why don't you write for me?' I asked, prompting her to lift her head from her notebook and sit upright to face me.

'Write for you?' She laughed.

'You've never written a poem for me.'

She tucked her hair behind her ear. 'I'm too frightened to.'

'Frightened?' I raised an eyebrow.

'Because I don't want to ruin it. I don't think I'd do you justice.' She shook her head and giggled as she looked down, embarrassed, and tugged on her jumper.

As I lifted her chin up between my thumb and finger, to meet my eyes, she smiled, almost apologetically. 'I think I love you.'

A smile couldn't help but appear on my face, and I leaned over until my lips met hers. I kissed her hard, her face between my hands, slowly sliding my fingertips into her hair, her hands on top of mine. My forehead pressing against hers, I reluctantly opened my eyes as she pulled away.

'I know I love you,' I said softly, staring deep into her sea green eyes. I rested my lips on her temple, gently.

'Chris?'

'Yeah?' I answered.

'Are you ashamed of me?'

It wasn't a question I would have expected at that exact time. It came out of the blue, but it hit me like a punch in the stomach. My face began to flush with guilt. If I was being totally honest with her, and myself, I wasn't exactly proud to be seen with her.

The whole online page had turned into a shitstorm, and almost overnight Isobel Finnie had become the most hated girl in the city. The messages thrown at her were like poison, yet she seemed unfazed. But when my name was slightly mentioned, I crumbled.

I didn't want to be hated by association, so when people brought up her name in conversation, I would fall quiet.

Our relationship was virtually a secret. I hadn't introduced her to any more of my friends, although they knew who she was. I played the whole situation as if it had been a one-night stand, a drunken mistake, a regret.

In another life, she would be the girl I would post all over my social media. She would have been the girl I would have taken to every single stupid old bar to show her off to people I barely knew. We would have been the couple everyone spoke about: 'They are so perfect for each other', 'Do you see the way he looks at her?', 'He is punching above his weight'. Isobel was the girl I had once dreamed of being with. She was the girl that I wanted to be mine. But now that she was mine, it could never be in the way I had dreamt it would.

'What makes you ask that?' I asked, dropping my eyes to my book. I couldn't act clueless and look at her; it would have torn me up.

'You don't really take me out. And I know you haven't told your friends about me—'

'I'm a private person, Isobel,' I snapped at her. I know I shouldn't have; she was right. But my defence was up, and it broke my heart to think that Isobel had found a flaw within me.

'There's a difference between being private and being secretive,' she said quietly.

I took her face in my hands again and looked into her eyes. Beneath the cold exterior that she had put up to mask her upset, I could clearly see hurt. 'I love you, Isobel, isn't that enough for you?'

She placed her hands on top of mine and slid them away from her face. 'I think the question is, am I enough for you?'

Yes. You are enough. You are everything and so much more. But you are the type of girl to make fire out of air. You are the type of girl my dad warned me about. You are a wildfire that can't be controlled. What kind of man does it make me if I spark a fire that I can't put out? I'll be the one that gets burned.

'Do you fancy something to eat?' I asked, seemingly abruptly.

'What?'

'Let's go out for something to eat.'

Isobel scrunched up her face, confused. 'Are you serious?'

'Isobel, you're right.' It hurt me to admit that I was wrong. 'Let me take you out.'

Her face lit up with excitement like a little puppy, and she took my hand as I stood up.

I took a deep breath and told myself to *man up*. She was a girl who deserved the world; the least I could do was be seen with her in public.

We walked through the cobbled lanes, breathing in the smell of fading summer air. The sky painted blood orange, the horizon looked as if it had been set on fire. The August heat had faded into a September cool. My favourite kind of weather; jumper weather.

Her hand was clasped inside mine, our fingers intertwined like a knot. In another world, I would have been as proud as punch to be seen with her. But I felt strangers' eyes crawl over us, like spiders creeping over our bodies. The streets began to fill up with whispers. People hissed at us. I finally realised how hard this must have been for her, on her own.

Isobel fell quiet as we approached a group of people around our age. I had no idea who they were, but they made it clear that they recognised us. As their eyes dragged up and down Isobel's body, the girls sniggered, and the boys glued their eyes to her. They wanted to unsettle her with their cruel judgments; there was no attempt at hiding it.

Isobel's eyes lit up with rage then fell to the ground. She didn't want to dare their gazes to a conflict she couldn't win. They only wanted her to react, for another thing to post about and spark the social media lynching.

As we passed them, one of them coughed. 'Bitch.'

Heat began to bubble and my chest tightened. The rage began to fester within me and I wanted to hurt him. But before I had the chance to even compose myself, Isobel ripped her hand from mine and whipped around to march into the boy's face.

'And what?' she challenged.

The boy's face went red and he looked to his friends for back-up, but they were struggling to pick their jaws from the floor.

'Well, go on. I'm a bitch and what?'

He attempted to sneer at her, trying to conceal the shock. 'And... and...' He had obviously not expected any response from Isobel and was struggling to find words.

His friend stepped in, slightly taller than him. Blond hair struck up to make him seem taller, his shoulders were broad and he towered over Isobel. I was scared and didn't know what do to. If it came to it, I would never have been able to fight him.

'I'll tell you what you are.' He smirked with every intention of intimidation, yet Isobel showed nothing more than her poker face. 'You're an evil and obviously mentally unstable little girl who set that church on fire.'

Isobel scoffed, 'I didn't do it.'

'Then little girls like you shouldn't be playing with fire. Bitches get burnt.'

She smiled, seemingly untroubled, and flicked her hair in his face, marching away and sliding her hands back into mine. Defiance in silence.

Her strength had left me speechless. She was able to stare into the face of a man who wanted to silence her and could still shout, without using words. She was fearless. She breathed fire when confronted, like a dragon defending the princess locked away inside of her. She had pretty big balls to do that.

8

Isobel

Tying my hair back from my face with a black velvet scrunchie, I wandered into my living room. In front of the TV, Dallas was bent over with her head in her hands.

'Dallas?' I asked.

She didn't need to answer. The TV already did.

> *Police investigating the murder of a girl whose body was found burned in a forest, just outside of Edinburgh, have appealed to the public for more information. Alison Duncan was an 18-year-old student, who had just started her first year at Edinburgh University, studying history. She was found in an area of grassland on Thursday morning. Police have confirmed that they are not ruling out a possible connection to the murder of Helen Gowdie, who sustained similar injuries.*

I inhaled deeply before gathering the courage to speak again. The silence between Dallas and me was deafening. Girls our age were being picked off one by one, and although we stayed quiet, the fear we shared was shattering. But this murder hit a little closer to home. Alison had been on Dallas's course.

'Did you know her?' I asked sheepishly.

'We had been on a few nights out together during Freshers.' Dallas rubbed her eyes to remind herself she was awake. 'She started sitting with us during lectures. I didn't know her well, but she was lovely, Isobel. She was so lovely.' Her face fell back into her hands as she began to cry.

I took a seat beside her and offered her a comforting arm. 'I'm sorry.'

'Have you seen what they have been saying about her?' Dallas managed to speak through sobs.

I pulled out my phone and typed Alison Duncan into Twitter. It was like *déjà vu*. She was branded a slut, a bitch. But there was something slightly different to Helen's death; something new that twisted my stomach.

Photos of Alison with her skin burnt to a crisp.

She lay limp, surrounded by grass towering above her and white roses. There was almost nothing left of her, just bones charred purple. On each photo of her body, there was a caption with the #liar.

'What did she lie about?' I asked Dallas.

'She said she had been raped by a boy on our course.' She sniffled. 'They were sort of seeing each other, but she said he took it too far one night. He seemed like such a nice boy, Isobel.' Dallas looked at me with embarrassment and realisation in her eyes. 'It was hard to believe, he was just so lovely.'

I didn't need to hear any more to know what had gone on. Every girl knows another girl with a similar story. All girls know someone who has been raped; yet no boys know a rapist. For Alison to come out with her story must have been incredibly difficult, yet the world didn't believe her.

The photos made my skin crawl and my throat tighten. Any sadness I had felt was overshadowed by the rage bubbling within me.

'I can't even read any more. I feel sick,' Dallas croaked. 'I just want this to be over.'

'We need to do something.' I got up to get my jacket and started tying the wire black laces of my boots round my feet, yanking hard.

'Where are you going, Isobel?' Dallas asked.

'I'm sick of not speaking,' I stated as I marched out of the door.

It was becoming clear that the girls who had been murdered were young women that someone wanted rid of. Someone wanted to shut them up. But Dallas and I would not allow their deaths to silence them. It was clear that both girls had had something to say, something someone feared. We didn't know what they wanted to say, but we wouldn't let it disappear.

Dallas followed me through the door, grabbing her coat. With anger pumping through our veins and resilience in our hearts, we marched through the cobbled lanes. Picking up a few supplies on our way, we marched to Castlehill and planted ourselves down.

We threw the canvas we had bought on the ground. Dallas shook the spray paint can and handed it to me. With my tongue between my teeth and sheer concentration painted on my face, I wrote what we needed to say. *You cannot burn away what has always been alight. We know the truth.*

With a picket sign in our hands, we sat cross-legged in the street, claiming the space as ours, not backing down to anyone who crossed us. The air was hot and the sun burned bright. It was a sign of rebellion. Two girls taking up space that no-one wanted them to have.

A girl came towards us, her eyes lit with curiosity. 'What youse doing?' she asked confidently. Her hand was in the back pocket of her denim jeans, a matching denim jacket thrown over her shoulder. She had to be one of the coolest girls I had ever seen.

'You know the two girls who were murdered?' Dallas asked.

'Uh-huh.' The girl nodded.

'We just want to show that we aren't scared of who did this to them. The girls obviously had something to say that someone didn't like, so they were killed. If they can't say it, we need to.'

The girl smirked in approval and nodded again. 'Cool,' she said, and sat down cross-legged beside us.

She was the first. Then there was another, and another, and another. As if within a blink of an eye, we had about thirty women, sitting cross-legged at the top of Castlehill. Chants began to break out from us. *We will not be silenced. We will not be silenced.*

Cameras started to flash in our faces, cheers erupted as our phones pinged with people tagging us in pictures of ourselves. Word of our protest travelled through the air, jumping from phone to phone. Every social media profile was lit up with comments about what we were doing. Comments came flooding into our inboxes.

A news van, with a satellite on its roof, came speeding up the street. A man dressed in a shirt and trousers fell out of his van, followed by a team with filming equipment.

'Can we speak to someone?' He was shouting at us before he even reached where we sat.

Collectively, most of the women turned their head towards me. My face went red with the embarrassment of all eyes being on me, but I accepted that the duty of the press would have to fall on me or Dallas. However, she looked at me, shook her head, and mouthed *no chance.*

I stood up and said, 'I can, I guess.'

The journalist's eyes lit up with my agreement. 'Great, what's your name?'

'Isobel,' I replied. 'Isobel Finnie.'

He reporter adjusted his tie while another microphone hovered above me and a camera was shoved inches from my face. The reported edged closer towards me, and the man behind the camera gave a thumbs up.

'This is Stuart Clancy, reporting live from Castlehill in Edinburgh. I'm here with Isobel Finnie, the girl who started this protest. Now, Isobel, can you tell me what is happening here?'

'Well, it started off as me and my roommate wanting to bring awareness about the murder of our friend—'

'Alison Duncan,' the reporter interrupted.

'Yeah, well. Alison was murdered by someone who wanted to shut her up. Just like they wanted to shut Helen Gowdie up. We're here today to show whoever murdered them that we will not shut up.'

When the interview wrapped up, Stuart thanked me for taking part. I thanked him for reporting us and getting the word out, before checking my phone. One after one, the tweets came flooding in:

We wish you would shut up.

Bossy bitches.

Feminazis.

Take a day off.

I had to chuckle to myself; people were so brave behind the screen. We were the ones who were actively going out and standing up for what was right. We were doing something, and they had nothing better to do than tear us down. People wouldn't say these things to my face.

Or at least, I didn't think so.

Settling back into my place within the group of girls, a man crossed our path, spitting at our feet. I tried to stand up to protest his vulgar act of disapproval, but Dallas put her arm over me to prevent me getting into an argument.

'You will never win with people like that,' she said. I wished she'd let me try.

As night fell, the group grew thinner. The colder the night grew, the less of us stood. The number of girls diminished one by one, and when it was only Dallas and I left, we decided to go home. Our message had been heard.

Cameron came to pick up Dallas. As she got into the car, she asked if I would be okay walking home myself. I said it was only a few blocks, so I would be fine. I waved them goodbye and started on my path home.

The cool night air breezed through my hair, swirling around my skin, and the sky was painted in lilac as the sun disappeared from the sky. I walked through the streets of Edinburgh and I cried.

I wept with frustration that I wasn't able to do something for her. Alison had died. There was no future for her. Her life had been taken from her. I didn't have the words to express my anger that someone had taken her life from her. I didn't know her, but she could have been a friend. She could have been me. I didn't have the words to express the sadness that I felt because she was gone.

Grief is only love with nowhere to go. It fills the hollow hole in your heart. I hadn't known Alison, but I knew Dallas was distraught. I wanted to tell her that the immense pain she felt would eventually become a dull ache. But I didn't know when that day would come, and I didn't know what to do until then.

A part of my soul had been ripped from me when Alison died. Hope had died. Alison didn't just die; she had been brutally murdered. And Helen had, too. There was no happy ending. I couldn't say they were in a better place or they were at rest, because I knew the truth. I knew that wherever they were, they were disturbed. Screaming, ripping out their hair, trying to get back to where they belonged.

As though we had been plunged back into the Middle Ages, we were living in fear. Women were being murdered one by one, in a desperate attempt to silence them. I began to think about the Witch Trials.

It was not something we were taught about in school. It was something I'd had to go and research myself to find out what I wanted. The trials were born out of sexism, the justification of the murders of women that were a little too loud, a little too sexual, a little too rich... a little too much.

As I walked on through the city, I realised how corrupt it all was. Leaflets advertising ghost tours, glamourizing the death of the witches that were murdered. Tourist attractions and open theatre productions turning these women into urban legends, like something out a horror film. I realised this was not home.

I didn't belong here with these people that I didn't trust. The cobble stones were stained with the blood of innocent women, murdered at the hands of their own communities. The air was polluted by the stench of death. We capitalised on murder, promoting these deaths as folklore and scary stories to tell our children. The Witch Trials were not a Hallowe'en costume. Witches didn't die; real women did.

I had never considered my own home to be a God-fearing city. However, with the threat of change, we had retreated into our old unjust morals. The same morals we had in the 16th century. If there was a God, how could he watch his people burn? If he hadn't abandoned us with the first witch trials, he had abandoned us now. God had forsaken us, not prepared to witness us brutally murdering each other. Humans had become a race of war, ravaging the planet of its beauty and bringing humanity to the brink of destruction; why would he stay to watch his own creations burn?

We would wash our hands of Helen and Alison's blood and hold hands with each other, in order to forgive ourselves for what sin we had committed here. We would beg for forgiveness but would not be sorry. We had dragged hell into our world in hope for heaven. There were some things that only God can forgive; this was not one.

I was so deep in thought that I had lost awareness of my surroundings. A hand from behind was placed over my mouth and a strong arm dragged me into an alleyway. My screams were muffled behind his sweaty palms, and my kicking did nothing to fend him off. Panic began to well up within me the more I begged myself to stay calm. The worst possible situations were playing in my head, like a gruesome horror film playing on repeat.

My breathing grew into hyperventilating, and I feared for my life. My eyes frantically darted around, trying to recognise the situation or find a face. I realised there were three or four other men, with their faces covered, surrounding me. The darkness of the night concealed their faces from me. Underneath their balaclavas, I couldn't even make out an eye colour.

I mentally prepared myself the worst while I struggled against his force, throwing my legs and trying to scream through his hand.

'Shut up, bitch!' he hissed in my ear.

He removed his hand from my mouth and threw me against the concrete.

'Listen, I don't have any money on me. I can take you to my flat. Here, take my phone. I won't tell anyone,' I pleaded with them in a desperate attempt for my life. I was trying to bargain with them, although I realised they might have more sinister intentions.

'Consider this a warning, Isobel.' One spoke while his friend held me down.

He pulled out a knife and dangled it in my face before pricking the skin of my cheek with the tip of the blade. I cried out in pain as I felt the blood trickle down my face. I raised my hand to feel the cut; it was only small but felt deep.

'Little girls should know their place. Don't be poking around or making a scene. You don't want us to know your name. Didn't Daddy tell you that little girls that play with fire get burnt?'

I didn't dare open my mouth.

The man holding me down freed me from his grip and I took the opportunity to sprint. I started running as fast as I could, too frightened to turn my head over my shoulder to see if they were following me. I threw myself through the door of my flat, holding back tears as I heard Dallas shouting from the kitchen.

'Yeah, that's me in,' I replied. 'I'm just going for a bath.'

I wasn't going to tell her or anyone what had happened. Everything was so out of control. I didn't want anyone else to get hurt. I had gone too far already.

As I settled myself into the burning water, I began to sniffle. I looked at my legs, prickled with little hairs, poking out of the cloudy water. As the water swirled around me, consuming me in heat, I submerged myself.

The water covered me like a transparent blanket of safety, protecting me from the world above, and I wished I could stay there forever. My dark hair surrounded me, floating in the water like a black rain cloud. It was an effort to raise myself out of the water, breaking free of its comfort. As I sat up, I raised a handful of water out of the bath and allowed it to slip through my fingers. And I sobbed.

Hot tears scorched my skin. Breathless, I couldn't swallow the lump that was wedged in my throat like a hot coal. My tears branded me with the burning pain I felt internally. The pain exploded in my chest, like fireworks, bursting inside of me and scorching my ribs. I grabbed hold of my chest in an attempt to contain the agonising pain of my heart ripping apart. Or what was left of it.

I felt trapped beneath my skin, in a body that I felt did not belong to me. I didn't like the person I had displayed to the world. *Was I just born bad? Was it my luck? What did I do to deserve it all?* If what they said was true and that I was an evil person, then I wanted to kill the girl within me. I just didn't know how to fix it.

It all became too much. My world was just too heavy to hold on my shoulders. I used to be like water – free and strong, yet soft. Now I was just drowning. I let my lungs catch fire and my heart exploded. I was consumed with self-hatred and it festered in every cell in my body. There was nothing poetic about pain; just an ache in my thighs and a storm in my mind.

They had won. I had lost. I was broken; I had fallen apart and I didn't have the energy to put myself back together again.

9

Chris

I knocked on the door and Dallas answered. 'Hi Chris,' she said, standing in the doorway. 'I'm just heading out. Izzie is in the bath.'

'No worries, I'll wait for her.'

I got the feeling that Dallas wasn't my biggest fan. I never sensed any feeling of warmth from her, but I couldn't blame her. I had hidden my relationship with her best friend for months, and I doubt Dallas would think I had stood up for her We didn't talk much to each other.

I planked myself down on the couch and flicked through TV channels.

'She probably won't be long, Chris. She's been in there for ages,' Dallas shouted as she left, the door slamming behind her.

I turned down the TV to shout through to Isobel as she was taking so long. As the volume decreased, I heard her wailing like the wind. I rushed up from the couch and lightly pushed the bathroom door open to reveal Isobel in the bath, naked and shivering.

She was painful to look at. Her spine protruded from her back, as if begging to break free from her skin. Her head was between her knees, with her shoulders jolting as she sobbed Her wet hair, hung over her back, was thin, her gaunt face like a skeleton of herself. She'd had her innocence ripped from her, and all that was left was a broken doll. She had been played with, used and abused, now thrown away.

I knelt beside the bath. I realised there was nothing I could say or do to take this pain from her, and it killed me inside. It took all the strength I had within me not to cry with her. The most impossibly heart-breaking experience in the world is watching someone you love fall apart, holding the pieces to put her back together yet the pieces just don't fit any more. They aren't the same person, and never will be. Their experience will either shape them or leave them broken forever.

I let her cry, her tears hitting the bath water like rain to a puddle. I couldn't even begin to understand how she felt. The world was against her; she only had herself and me.

Eventually, her sobs began to diminish, and she sniffed and splashed her face with some of the cooling bath water. I stayed still.

'I need to go, Chris,' she said quietly, still sniffling. Her voice was thick with emotion.

'Let's go to mine,' I suggested. 'We can stay there for a bit—'

She cut me off with heartbreak in her eyes. 'No, Chris. I need to leave.'

A hard thud slapped within my chest; I felt my heart shatter as I realised what she meant.

'Go where, Isobel?' My voice began to tremble. I already knew the answer.

'I don't know. I might just go home.'

'Where's home, Isobel?'

She could move halfway across the world and it would never be enough. Her reputation would follow her no matter what. The memories of what she'd faced were branded into her mind, preventing her from seizing any opportunity, in fear that she wasn't good enough. The problem wasn't the hate she received; it was the damage it had done to her self-worth. 'Don't let them win,' I begged.

'They've already won!' She began to raise her voice. 'Don't you see? They have already won!'

'Isobel, it's not only you. I'm hurting, too.'

'You're hurting?' Her voice started to crack. 'Oh yeah, I'm sure it's so hurtful having to be embarrassed of your girlfriend. It's such a shame for you that I'm so hated.' She was belittling me with her sarcastic tone, yet her eyes pleaded for some mercy.

'I know it's hard, Isobel. I know you think everyone hates you and you're struggling with it all, but I can fix it.'

'Get this out your fucking head!' she snapped. 'I am not some perfectly damaged girl that you can fix! I am not this broken fantasy you have conjured in your mind!'

'What? You going to fix yourself? You're not doing a good job so far.' It was a low blow and I almost regretted the words as soon as they fell from my lips. But they were out there, and I was too stubborn to go back.

'I'm trying!' she screamed at me. 'I'm trying so hard, why can't you see that?'

'Why can't you let me in?'

'You don't understand.'

'Aw, I give up Isobel. Nothing I do is good enough for you.'

'No, it isn't! And what? Why am I the bad guy because I know my worth?'

'You should consider yourself lucky!' I shouted.

Isobel looked like I had slapped her across the face. The tears began to form in her eyes and her lip started to quiver. She closed her eyes and took a deep breath to compose herself. But I knew I had struck her in a way I never should have.

'Please get out,' she whispered, her eyes still closed.

'You're being ridiculous.' I said, half-laughing. I hoped she would see sense, laugh and fall back into my arms, and let me look after her.

The water spilled over the edge as she tore up the water and stood up, naked, in the bath. 'Get the fuck out.'

She didn't want looked after. So, I left.

10

Isobel

He was gone, and I was alone.

My chest felt empty, as if he had reached in and ripped out my heart. I hated myself for feeling like that. I despised how I'd relied on him; I'd just wanted him to make things better and just to fix it all for me. I had allowed myself to fall for him, but instead of catching me, he'd let me hit the ground.

I'd felt so safe around him, as if he could protect me from anything. It was too much to expect from him, I know. But being at battle with the world, I'd hoped I had someone to defend me, or at least be on my side.

The realisation that I was and always would be on my own was just so much to handle. The consciousness of reality was crushing.

I climbed out the bath, my wrinkled skin dripping with cold droplets, then wrapped myself in a towel and walked, barefoot, to my room. I slipped a white nightie over my head as I tried to hold back the tears that were already running down my face.

I just didn't know how much longer I could keep up this fight against the world. I was exhausted. Raising my arms to slide into my nightie was a real effort. I just wanted to collapse into bed and sleep until it was all over.

I wrapped the duvet covers around me, hoping they would shelter me from the world outside. The guilt in my chest was crippling; I thought there must be something that I had done to deserve it. Thoughts were pounding against my head: of running way; of hurting myself; of ending it all. I was desperate for some sort of relief.

I was a shell of a girl. I didn't know even who I was. I had always prided myself on being kind, but now I had all these people telling me I was evil. It was as if there was someone inside of me, begging to come out, but I just didn't know how to convey the real me to the world.

There was nothing left to feel. My heart hurt to carry. A part of me wished I wouldn't wake up from this sleep. I could survive what was happening to me, but I didn't know if I could survive my mind.

I heard my door open and footsteps in the hall. I didn't have the energy to say 'hello' to Dallas or to tell her what had happened. I'd pretend I was asleep if she shouted in. I feared that if I opened my mouth, I would just sob.

I realised that the tapping on the floor was more than one person's footsteps. Dallas must have brought her boyfriend home. I sighed and rolled over in bed, slightly annoyed. I had no reason to be irritated but I just wanted to be alone.

With their arrival, they made some racket. It sounded as if they were falling into things, knocking things over, bouncing around. They couldn't have been drunk; Dallas had only left around an hour ago.

When the noises continued, I shouted through, 'Do you want to shut up? I'm trying to sleep.'

The footsteps became louder and quicker, marching towards me. I kept myself buried under the covers but fear began to beat in my chest. I heard my door burst open and I knew that it wasn't Dallas who was standing at the end of my bed.

My covers were torn off me, and without even looking to see who these men were, I jumped up and darted towards my door. One of them grabbed my foot, forcing my body to hit the ground. I screamed before a hand was slapped over my mouth. Using my free foot, I kicked up to hit any part of the man who held me down. He didn't even seem to flinch. I struggled underneath him, looking at the feet of the two other men who stood in front of me.

I closed my eyes and tried to wake up from this nightmare, but when I opened my eyes again, they were still there.

11

Chris

I dismissed my phone as I turned on the radio. The cheerful voice filled my bedroom with an excitement. 'It is 9.30pm on a miserable Friday, people, but we have just the songs to brighten up your night.' The sounds became cloudy after that, as I tried to make sense of the day.

I had slept since the night before, when it had all kicked off with Isobel. Before the clouds could clear from my eyes, I logged on to Facebook. The bright light from my phone screen illuminated my face, slightly stinging my eyes. I sighed as I scrolled down my feed, unable to avoid the toxins written on Isobel's profile.

'Slut, slag, skank.' The usual insults spat at her through screens. 'Bitch.' As difficult as it was to admit, I had become almost desensitised to it all. 'Fucking witch.'

Knowing what those words were doing to her, I began to feel physically ill.

I turned my phone off and crawled out of bed. The ache in my bones restricted me from moving freely, so I slowly guided my body to reach yesterday's jogging trousers that hung, dead, over my chair. They clung to my skin as I pulled them on.

Barefoot, I stumbled to the bathroom, only to see the rain. My ears rang as the rain smacked the windows with the heavy force of a thousand years, clinging to the glass, begging for me to let it in.

A feeling of being dirty came over me. I felt unclean in my own skin, like a sickness crawling over me.

I stepped into the shower and let the hot water burn my skin, wrenching the nightmare out of me. As I turned the water off, I paused for a moment and allowed the diminishing drops to hit my face; I wasn't quite ready to leave its comfort.

When I found the courage to leave, I went back to my room and dressed then made my way out.

Standing in the doorway, watching the rain fall, dismay curled up within me. The rain poured from the dark skies above me. The black, shrivelled clouds cried vigorously, their tears striking the ground like glass. The brisk air bit my face as I stepped out into the hail.

As I darted towards my bike, a gleam from my phone lighting up caught my eye and a familiar eerie feeling crept over my body as I looked at my screen.

With a shaking hand, I lowered my hood to look. Through the falling raindrops, I saw hundreds of comments tagging me on a livestream video.

In the video, there was a girl wearing a white dress underneath the rope that restrained her to a large wooden post. A few men stood around her, dressed in black hoodies, pouring a clear liquid over her. She was soaked, as if she had drowned. Her hair hung like rope over her pale face. It was impossible to tell if the rain had drenched her, or if it was her own tears. Looking up to the sky, she began to scream, her painful cries shredding through the crisp, autumn air.

The sight of her halted me in my path and turned me to stone. I was frozen, forced to look at her as a flock of crows cried above me. I instantly recognised the location as Castlehill. Blood red autumn leaves started to swirl around her, dancing at her feet. Her green eyes looked directly at the camera, and with all the might she had in her body, her hand tore through the rope to try and free herself. Isobel Finnie.

Terror rushed through my body. My heart thudded against my tight skin like a drum, as if trying to burst from my chest. My breath shortened as my body began to shut down in a panic. I couldn't control my breathing. It was impossible to fight the instinct that drew me towards the bike. The twist in my gut led my feet into the pedals, and I began to cycle. As fast as I could.

The white tires, blackened with mud, ripped through the crumbling road. Over little rocks, the bike screeched, painted with a blood red glaze. Faster and faster, the bike tore through the rain, slashing through the streets of Edinburgh in a desperate attempt to escape. As the white basket disintegrated into ash, I cried out for the bike to go on.

Skidding round sharp corners like a flash, I cycled. I knew the trail; I followed the same path as I would in my dreams. The adrenaline was bubbling in my chest, through my arms, to my pedalling feet.

As far as I could tell, there was nothing chasing me. There was only the force pulling my body to the top of Castlehill.

I cycled through the city until a realisation stopped me dead. My feet slammed on the ground to balance the bike as I observed that the streets of Edinburgh seemed empty. At six o'clock on a Friday evening in Scotland's capital city, there was no-one. Deprived of souls, Edinburgh was dead. Not a single soul haunting the streets. Only the smell of burning smoke, stuffing my nose with ash.

I couldn't tell where the fire was coming from, but the smoke surrounded me. Grey ash clouds swam through the narrow lanes, the overwhelming smell forcing coughs to splutter from my mouth.

Then I heard it. A blood-curling scream pierced the air. My heart halted. I stopped breathing. Screams of terror rang like sirens in the darkness and I started cycling towards the cries, adrenaline accelerating me up the steep slope leading to Castle-hill.

Through the smoke, I saw her.

Her name escaped my mouth as the bike fell from my grasp. Beneath the tears in her gaze was fear. Desperation. For the first time in my life, I saw Isobel allowing herself to be vulnerable. She didn't have a solution. She didn't know what to do, apart from hope that someone would see sense. She hoped that someone would save her because, for the first time ever, Isobel Finnie couldn't save herself.

She reached out towards me, emitting a terrible scream that tore me apart. My eyes scanned frantically for a face, but I saw none. The crowds were present, but they were invisible. Hidden behind screens, I could still feel the heat from the fire in their eyes. Hundreds, if not thousands, of men, women, and children, thirsty for blood. I could picture the rage spitting from between their teeth as they typed their chants on the livestream. *Burn the bitch. She deserves it. Glad to see her go. Fucking ugly skank.* There were no fists of fury pumping in the hot, dangerous air, only angry thumbs typing away.

She struggled beneath the rope that restrained her, grunting. With her chin pointed at the dark clouds above, I saw her lips. They were stained red with blood, bitted in desperation as she had struggled to free herself. From a distance, she looked like an angel, dressed in nothing but a white nightgown and surrounded by a yellow glow.

But with closer inspection, it became clear to me that the dress was spoiled with the dark ash of the smoke, coming from the torches of the men dressed in black. Mascara ran down her face, merging with her lipstick of blood. The yellow glow had transcended into harsh flames surrounding her. The murder of an angel who had been dragged from heaven.

'Are you mad?' her voice squealed. The fearless façade had fallen, and she was left begging for her life.

I couldn't believe what I was witnessing, the fire in their eyes. I felt as though I had been plunged into the medieval ages, times of insanity. They were burning a girl alive. A nineteen-year-old girl was being brutally murdered in front of me, because of a burned church. We had all lost our minds.

A weight dragged me to the ground as I tried to run towards her. A man jived towards me, knocking me to the floor. My head smacked the concrete, and as I touched where the pain was coming from, I was met with blood. The man continued to hold me there.

Desperate to reach her, my throat was torn with the screams of her name. I struggled underneath the weight of the man in an attempt to reach her, until two others moved to help him control my struggle.

Fear's hand gripped tight around my throat, and I was paralysed with revulsion. With my lungs raw with screams of terror and tears in my eyes, I was forced to watch her fight.

She continued to struggle, as the rage inflamed within me. I spat as I shouted, my heart racing as I tried to hold back furious tears. The smoke stung my eyes, causing them to water. I screamed, pleas of mercy, begging them to stop.

A man, dressed in nothing more than blue-washed jeans and a black hoodie, stood up to the podium beside where Isobel was trapped. His beard was shaggy, untidy, and he had violence in his eyes. He couldn't have been more than ten years older than me, but his presence unsettled me.

Taking the phone from his accomplice's hand, he spoke directly into the camera.

'Our city has been terrorised. We have been coerced by women like Helen Gowdie, Alison Duncan, and now Isobel Finnie. We refuse to let our home and our people be bullied by these evil spirits any longer. Therefore, Isobel Finnie, you have been found guilty of witchcraft and sentenced to death.'

It was too late. The torch carrying furious flames was lowered to the wood, and the fire crawled rapidly along until it met Isobel's dress. As the dancing flames climbed up the garment, she let out a dreadful cry. The stench of burning flesh poisoned the air as her skin melted from her.

They had won.

There was nothing peaceful about it. She struggled and kept struggling, like a little spark trying to escape the flames, but the fire was too ferocious and dragged her back in. Her pleading eyes were unrecognisable under her charred skin. Her gorgeous complexion was scorched, leaving nothing but purple skin hanging from her bones.

I watched the life go from her as her struggle finally ended. Her head fell from being upright and jerked to her chest. The tension in her body was at rest.

They had gotten what they had come for, but there were no cheers from the spectating audience. There was no clapping or laughing. All that haunted the atmosphere was the realisation that a young girl had been murdered at the hands of a bloodthirsty crowd. The realisation that a nineteen-year-old girl had been executed for witchcraft, without a trial or viable evidence. There was only the realisation that we, as a society, had marked the beginning of the dark ages. We had been plunged into our society, three hundred years earlier.

What started as rumours had transcended into accusations, which then became a witch trial. A comprehensive, outright witch trial. We had murdered a girl, suspecting her of being possessed by some sort of dark magic.

I wish I could tell you that Isobel Finnie died in a heroic blaze of glory. I wish I could say she held a defiant smile as the flames consumed her. I wish I could say she didn't stop fighting until the fire burnt out, and she survived the flames that ate at her skin. But she didn't.

She cried for survival but begged for death, pleading for the excruciating pain to end. Her eyes were wide with terror and she reverted to the scared little girl within her. She was desperate to find eyes to hold onto, a friendly face. But I got there too late.

There was nothing peaceful about her struggle. She gasped for air through the smoke that drowned her, and the smell of her own burning skin singed in her nose. She screamed dreadful screams that will haunt me until the day I die.

As she wailed through the wind, begging for her life, the man who had lit the flame said, 'A girl who sets the world on fire has to burn with it.'

The Vengeance of King Martoon

James McGunnigle

1

King Martoon's raid

There over in South America, there a small poor town called Guntershill appears to be a little skinny Monkey who was seven years old. He lives with his family whilst in the presence of school within a group of friends who adores him to his best caring. Usually after school they would hang out beside a bench that sits on a tall hill surrounded by palm trees.

The first thing that comes into their minds is the big military back yard as shown. Robin and his friends would always watch the army train every evening having to witness some of the weird drills these soldiers do, but overall, they have fun mocking them from the distance which makes the whole scenario hilarious if you think about it.

Robin stays in a creamy colour semi-detached house made with hard but smooth concrete with a front yard lined with banana trees and at the back yard shows a big jungle tree with swings covering the majority of the sunshine. The town is generally a jungle-like an overview blocking most light from burning Guntershill into black charcoal.

One early morning wasn't the usual routine, Robin arose from his bunk bed feeling ravenous and slowly walked outside the backyard to grab a banana considering the poor state of food provision his family could only afford. Robin walked back inside with the banana. He walked into the living room to turn on the television, but, when he went over to turn it on with the remote the door from the backyard slammed closed, Robin got a fright, Robin's four brothers had just woken from that loud bang sound Robin had just witnessed.

Robin's brothers come running downstairs quite disturbed but curious to find out what or who made that noise.

As soon as they saw Robin their faces instantly turned red and then they started screaming at him accusing him of being a trouble-maker sounding exaggerated as if they suddenly snapped going rogue.

Robin began explaining to his brothers that he was not the one to blame, his brothers refused to believe him considering what he does when his temper rises which result losing faith in him altogether because of Robin's anger issue every time he gets the blame even if it isn't his fault. Robin progressed from crabby to full-on arrogant when it comes to pointless arguments. Their parents suddenly got a huge fright, the father came downstairs to deal with the situation. Robin continued explaining what had happened, his brothers couldn't be bothered about his excuses, their father looked incredibly pissed at Robin himself and his other sons. Robin begged his father to listen to him for the first time, fortunately, Robin, however, his father didn't threaten him like he always did in the past family arguments. The father just locked the doors and windows and walked off disgruntled without helping Robin, but he did leave him alone with his brothers to resume their fight.

The brothers then felt confused and wondered why their father didn't do anything about it, Robin ran upstairs with his banana whilst his brothers watched him disappear into his room, but whatever, they didn't feel any regrets, the brothers all sat down watching the television about a robot that apparently went missing from area 51, they say that they're still trying to get clues of the mysterious criminal. Anyway, Robin ran into his room and slammed the door behind him, he froze in disbelief despite the fact that his arrogance has been caused by minor issues that made him overreact to those small mistakes because of his brother's moody reactions to whenever he does something stupid, Robin goes psycho and usually starts to make excuses to stop himself from being worse, but, it doesn't apply to his brothers and especially his parents.

Suddenly, one of the windows in Robin's room - that his father forgot to lock – was opened by big gushes of wind, Robin moved to close it but then he saw something outside of his home, almost everyone was standing outside their homes. He paused for a moment to address all these unusual things, on the contrary, he thought, it's a memorial remembrance tradition. Robin then started to overwhelm his thoughts of various possibilities on what this strange happening could've been, but it didn't last for long.

His mother shouted his name in a panicky tone, Robin ran downstairs again to see what was all the commotion about, after he dashed as quickly as he could to examine the curiosity that he's ever wondered, Robin saw the most intense mystery that any person will ever witnessed.

July 6th, 1995 (The mystifying retraction)
Everyone from all over Guntershill gathered together to see this giant ball of light floating above the ground. They all stared at

it. Robin and his brothers gasped slightly surprised, Robin began walking towards the apparition that seemed to hold a mysterious power, he kept walking slowly towards the glowing light, he could feel a tickle somewhere in his head that he could not process, he was curious to see what this light holds, he believes it might be a good sign.

After a moment of silence the glowing ball exploded with red fog which blocked all light from reality, Robin saw the light fading away from existence.

The fog continued to block the sky and sunlight. Robin's brothers ran over to him worried, he looked at them. His older brother suddenly reached his hand to grab Robin. Robin refused to listen to his family, so he walked forward, his brothers followed behind him to ensure his safety.

The sky was now covered in pure red fog, the sun dimmed by it. For a moment Robin started to regret attempting to run away from his family, he thought of his dream of becoming a leader of the army because that was his noble desire, his brothers still followed him and still had the guts to protect Robin.

Robin's father realised his four sons were missing, he turned over to his wife and told her that their sons weren't to be seen, the wife gasped in fear as the father had felt responsible meanwhile trying to calm her down and told her that he'll go and find them. The boys had heard their mother shouting their names including Robin. He and his brothers went over to their parents, their mother was devastated at first by shouting at them for wandering off without their supervision, however, as she calmed down a little she became more neutral to her four sons, the father, on the other hand, was pissed at them as well be he's less exaggerated than his wife.

The red fog out of nowhere began to draw into a ball, the fog clouds kept curling into the centre of the retraction force, everyone felt afraid at this moment, except Robin who didn't fear a bit. The fog suddenly started to glisten out light over in the centre of the retraction force, the light is so bright that it blinded Robin's eyes at the blink of a beam, Robin nearly tumbled onto the ground but his strength saved his balance within seconds. Everyone began slowly walking back into their houses but at the same time keeping a hawk's eye on the mysterious object. Robin thought of taking another step forward but then he got yanked by his dad, they went back into the house without hesitation they immediately slammed their front door.

Robin and his brothers all sat down on the family couch with their mother assertive and lightly aggressive but on the other hand, the father gets all nettled so he turned at his loving anti-depression beverage, the father left upstairs to get drunkard up in the attic of the house. The other boys felt much ashamed of themselves but got peeved at Robin at the same time as their mother was about to punish all four of her sons, they all heard a loud bang upstairs. Their mother paused and then began looking up to the ceiling curiously, Robin sat in a huff for a minute until his mother went upstairs to see Robin's dad. Robin sat with his arms crossed really annoyed at the situation, however, he did have a lot of questions he has in mind about the mystery of the ball that appeared out of the blue without any logical theories whatsoever. His brothers walked back into their rooms disgruntled, Robin sat alone in the living room with the news currently on.

He turned up the volume to hear the recent news, the reporter on the television began telling about a bunch of political issues. Robin yawned loudly for a minute until... The news reporter mentioned something about an undefined creature, it sounded ridiculous at first because he thought it was another alien hoax. He doubted the truth of it ever happening.

Robin tried to forget about that giant light ball that he witnessed earlier, the thought began to fall into his subconscious mind, Robin couldn't take away that fact that the giant fog ball somehow came into existence.

Robin continued to watch the news reporter talk more into detail about the creature, Robin had his arms wrapped around a blanket that he found under the table of the kitchen, he sat back onto the soft fluffy sofa cushions. Overall, Robin does like to have a laugh about the silliest drama that goes on in society, he seemed interested whenever something too good to be true comes on television.

His dad, out of nowhere, rambles into the kitchen looking around half asleep, Robin saw an empty bottle of beer that his dad was holding firmly with his right hand feeling anxious, Robin proceeds to walk in the kitchen.

Robin tiptoed over to his dad and tapped him on the shoulder, Robin asked his dad why he was like this? Robin's dad didn't listen and ignored him as if nothing had happened. He knew his father was drunk. He decided to escort his dad into his room and tucked him into bed, before walking out of his parent's room and going downstairs to watch the rest of the report before he went to sleep.

He sat down again and continued to watch the news until... It mentioned the giant fog ball that Robin could not get out of his thoughts. Disturbed, he didn't hesitate to turn off the television with the remote. Robin immediately fainted on the soft carpet floor and fell into a deep sleep.

July 7th, 1995 (The Raid of King Martoon)) (12:00)
Robin is still asleep, in his sleep he hears folk screaming, he feels lifted from the ground, he smells the fresh coffee on the house, he tastes the extraordinary natural flavour of bananas. All of a

sudden Robin slowly opened his eyes to see himself inside his room, he then slowly tilted his head over to the left to see his mother crying in tears and then he tilted his head over to the right to see his three brothers appalled.

He hesitated to say anything at this point, he had thoughts about what would happen if he awakened for a minute until he heard his brother say "We love you bro", the first time in Robin's life that he heard the most positive thing to ever hear, this meant a second chance for Robin to finally win his family back from the negativity that imposes onto them.

He decided it's time that he should surrender to the upcoming punishment he'll likely face, his family stopped to see slight movement coming from his arms, they gasped for a moment. Robin got up from his deep sleep confused, he could not process what happened yesterday with the nonsense that boggled his mind with perplexing unanswered mysteries that remains silent for which could almost be a possibility from its world of unreality.

Robin sat up from his bed rubbing his eyes, his brothers were relieved to see him, unfortunately, though, they were angry at Robin for scaring them to death of losing a brother of their family. Eventually, their mother calmed her three sons down, she then went over to Robin, she made a sigh for a moment until she confessed something to Robin that he will never forget.

"Son, I have to tell you something, I know you hate us denying things behind your back, but, it's just..." Robin's mother was about to finish her sentence, but, she suddenly got interrupted by her husband with a slurred argument, he was holding a litre of beer in his left hand and a cigarette in his right hand. "Got a light on yea, eh?" slurred Robin's dad, his wife suddenly pushed her husband into another room.

The boys heard a fight from the next room, meanwhile, Robin's brothers turned their backs away from Robin with their busty arms wrapped around them ignoring Robin's presence. Robin didn't approve either with their relationship together so he just got up from his bed and ran downstairs.

He walked into the living room feeling hopeless and a little depressed as he's the only being who ever was bullied throughout his life so far with his brothers. He sat down onto the couch, he reached for the remote to turn on the television again. Suddenly realising the television didn't have its power plug, he took the biggest tantrum ever to be made, starting with ripping the cushions into tiny bits of fluff. He ran into the kitchen and began snatching all of the bananas from the basket.

The next thing Robin knew, is his older brother Christopher, came downstairs with a camping bag strapped onto his back.

"Where are you going bro?" asked Robin with a grumpy face..

Christopher felt a slight concern for Robin. "The question is, why did you fall asleep onto the floor last night?" he asked.

Robin gave Christopher a skeptical look on his face feeling as if Christopher was hiding something, "I'm not stupid, you're running away from home aren't you?" asked Robin with his arms across his hips.

Christopher didn't look surprised by the fact that Robin held a suspicious thought about this insightful situation, so, he rolled his eyes along with a sigh. "Listen, I know you're afraid of losing your hopes on dad, but, you're the only one who can resolve the problem," said Christopher with despair.

Robin had no faith in Christopher no matter the way his interpretation was revealed to aim at, "Let me ask you something then, Christopher?" asked Robin, "when is this family going to start loving me like the old times, huh?" Robin firmly questioned Christopher for he had shown a lack of empathy for Robin, Christopher didn't even care at this point and reached for his brown rough leather jacket.

As soon as he opened the door Robin dropped his banana making a thump onto the floor, Robin marched towards Christopher huffing whilst he walked. "So, you're going to abandon us!?" as Robin demanded an answer from Christopher.

"Robin?" Christopher called, "remember this at the bottom of your heart..." Robin stood silent for a moment paused. "You now should protect the family, don't worry about me, we might cross the same bridge perhaps, in the future," said Christopher with sorrow, then waved his hand walking out of the house far away from home. Robin had finally lost all hope to reuniting the family.

July 7th, 1995 (The Raid of King Martoon)) (15:00)
Robin decided to chill outside to review his negative thoughts before sunset, there he stumbled outside the backyard, Robin sat down onto a wooden deck summer chair built with a fabric cover attached to the wooden structure.

He laid back under the big tree of shade, growing worse gradually as he feels more neglected as his time went on without Christopher. Overwhelmed by these compulsive thoughts that won't let go of his mind.

July 7th 1995 (King Martoon's Appearance)) (10:45 pm)
It is pitch black, the placid wind blows by the jungle trees swaying, up at the skies a full moon occurs in the appearance of tonight's shine, all lanterns lit up over at every house in Guntershill glaring orange-coloured lighting. Robin is already asleep, everything is unruffled and serene.

Eventually, something dropped into the bushes onto the backyard, it began moving around making weird squeaky sounds. Robin awakened from the squeaky sound, he's suspiciously cognisant, he didn't make one little move, instead, he let it come to him. He stood there as long as he could until the noise came to him. After five minutes of stillness, Robin decided to start rambling into the bushes to catch the sound, he felt fearless regardless his family taught him self-defence, he knew what to do when it comes to ambushes.

Robin kept quiet momentarily, he crawled through the bushes to camouflage himself from those ones who'd investigate the sound that Robin would most of the time anticipate, meanwhile, the sound kept getting more louder as it got darker. When it reaches pure pitch black, the wind goes cold, the clouds faded away showing the moon and stars. Robin looked around inside the bushes to approach closer to the squeaky sound, then, he saw a tail popping out of nowhere, the tail had red and yellow stripes, at the end of the tail had a sharp fat stinger.

Robin crept up on the tail whilst it moved smoothly, swishing gently as if the creature is making less movement. Robin kept quiet, he slowly lifted out his hand to grab it, it was too late, the tail got away. "Dang it!" mumbled Robin with a fixed grin of hate on his face.

Then, Robin suddenly decided to pop his head out of the bushes to scout for the creature he'd wanted to catch, he looked around, nothing in sight, Robin got annoyed by that, so, he decided he still wanted to catch it.

He made his move by running over to the big jungle tree in the middle of Guntershill, he looked around left to right, above and below his surroundings, still not any new incomers, however, he was still eager to capture this creature to please his camping friends.

Suddenly, Robin began hearing the squeaking sound again, this time, it was coming from everywhere! He didn't move an inch forward, this time, he started to copy the sound, he mimicked the exact tone, his version of the squeak was virtually the same as the one the creature made.

The creature stopped as the mimic sound was heard! Robin continued to repeat the sound multiple times, eventually, the sound stopped with an abrupt silence, a few minutes in, Robin stayed his ground as long as the creature remained in its ground position, then, Robin respectfully accepted to leave it some space for a while.

An hour had passed, and nothing had changed until a bright interruption shone onto Robin, there also he heard shouting, and finally realised who was out for him... His father stood opposite with a belligerent posture, his fists gripping firmly together getting ready to grab him and take him away into the house. "Son!!!, what on earth are you doing out here?!" Robin's father screamed.

"It's not what you think it is!" Robin pleasantly apologised to his father,

"In a situation like this son?! Are you really wanting to play games with me at this time of the night!?" shouted his father with anger.

Robin and his father kept arguing over the scenario, Robin began to urge his father to smooth the noise.

"Just you wait until your mother hears about this son!!" yelled his father and roughly yanked Robin's arm.

At that moment something popped out of the bushes!

"What the heck was that?!" Robin exclaimed!

His dad stared behind him. "You!! In the house right now!!" .

Suddenly, Robin abruptly sees a mysterious crowd of shadows surrounding him and his dad "What the... Who are you, what's your name? And why are you in our territory?" interrogated Robin's dad.

"I'm not here to have a feast with a couple of ignominious idiots! So, why don't you let us visit your little pitiful land of yours!?" said the mysterious creature.

"You need to ask our mayor! He'll be the one to ask, I'm just a citizen of this state!" Robin replied.

After a moment of standing around, the creature came forward out of the shadow. It had a black feather crown at his forehead, it had a long black and yellow stripy tail with a fan blade at the tip end, he was covered in cherry red fur.

"I'd be acquitted at this point, but... You just held the wrong person!" said the creature with little irony.

"What is this, a game or something!? I'm not going to sound the alarm if you don't take any more steps!" said Robin's dad.

Then, the creature and its minions slowly began backing into the forest that is at one of the ends of the town district. "Better be ready! You got an hour to gather the whole town including your leader!! Trust me, son of yours will see the tapestry of your skin under the grave of what used to walk in its two legs!" Then, the creature faded away into the forest.

Robin raged with anger at himself and the creature!

"You are dead to me Robin!!!" shouted his dad then walked off to sound the alarm.

Robin started to punch his fist onto a brick wall with all his anger and stress despite the fact the creature got away because of his drunken father who messed up his plan!

The alarm went off! Everyone gathered up at the assembly "Listen, regarding our festival celebration this year! Unfortunately, I just got told that a lot of intruders are preparing to raid our town!!" announced Robin's dad.

The mayor suddenly ran over to him "I heard it all! I'm going to make an urgent negotiation with army force to come!", the mayor quickly hopped away in panic!

An hour has passed, everyone still waited on the army for their rescue, out of nowhere, a red fire fog explosion appears in the forest! Everyone started to panic "where are they!!!" said the mayor, the intruder crowd began running through the fog towards Guntershill.

They arrived in the town exactly on time! "You had one chance to get prepared! I see that isn't the case! You will die under the insatiable majesty's last discern!!!".

All the red furry creatures began laughing in the slight of chuckles "That's pathetic! I thought I'd meet my rival, yet, you seem to be a threat to us all!" said the red creature.

All of a sudden, trucks and helicopters arrived behind the crowd! A man stepped out of the truck with haste "Stop in the name of the enforcement!" said the stranger. Everyone began to run outside the town, however, Robin didn't run, instead, he stood his ground!

"So... You must be one to vanquish, let me introduce myself!" said the red creature.

The stranger abruptly interrupted "King Martoon! Right? Don't remember me!? Well, Andrew's the name!"

Robin looked shocked with confusion! Soon, a mysterious crowd begins raiding Guntershill!

Everyone begins running into the forest far up ahead, Robin begins running as well, unfortunately, he realised that he's lost in the middle of a war against those nasty intruders, Robin followed everyone else, as he ran with the folk, he saw the man Andrew who stood up protecting Guntershill with a bunch of other soldiers.

Robin kept running as fast as he could until he reached up at the hill, King Martoon's minions surrounded him making him unable to escape their trap. Robin halted still, of a sudden... Andrew, the man came to rescue Robin from this disaster! Robin begins to notice the beginnings of a bond between him and Andrew already.

Andrew carried Robin on his shoulder and pushed the intruders aside with mighty thrust heading down from the hill, Robin couldn't process this wacky battle that he was in. Andrew then decided to head to his truck, he opened the front door "Get in! Don't worry about your parents, I'll get them on board!" said the soldier.

Robin sat in the truck for five minutes until he saw just Andrew, Andrew gets into the truck, he starts the engine, Robin looked confused, so, he questioned Andrew "What about my parents?" he said nervously.

Andrew didn't reply. Instead he drove the truck outside Guntershill, Robin was so confused, he didn't know how to process that or how to react!

Andrew drove for hours passed, Robin nearly fell asleep until Andrew said the most devastating thing that Robin would hear "Your parents died after running into the forest, apparently, it was the perfect trap!" said Andrew.

Robin couldn't believe what he heard at this moment "I have to ask, why didn't I go stick with them at the beginning, things would've been better back then!" he said.

Andrew looked at him for a moment in silence, then, he stopped the truck in the middle of an unknown street address "Listen, you are not like the rest, in fact... you'll regret saying that, besides, I'm the one who saved you!" he said abruptly

Robin scratched his head a couple of times.

Robin followed Andrew into which he calls his house. "What was that red furry animal that attacked my home?" asked Robin with curiosity.

"It's a long story, you'll understand once I die! Maybe you should make yourself a new home, try to adapt to the change, son!" said Andrew.

Robin took his shoes off, he put them on the shoe rack beside the front door, Robin walked onto the soft brown carpet in the living room, he laid onto a smooth fluffy black couch constantly thinking about what happened back there with all of the wacky nonsensical events that took place at Guntershill.

The soldier sat down beside Robin giving him a pat on the shoulder ."You are dauntless. Always speak your mind! don't let anyone bring you down, do you understand?" said Andrew.

"I'm really confused" cried Robin pouring many emotions all at once, not knowing what to react.

Andrew consoled Robin trying to calm him down with all his love, Andrew looked at Robin one more time as if he wanted to take him into adoption "You know what? I'm guarding this kid for life's potential! This is a new future for all of us... *He may be a monkey, but, for goodness sakes man, look at this tiny skinny boy with the greatest power of hope and an underestimated twist! He's... He's... He's like my son who died on my knees!*" mourned Andrew with the unthinkable sorrows drifting around his mind being washed away and returning back into his mind like the sea.

Now! Robin gets adopted by Andrew over in America, Annapolis Maryland. Robin had to spend the rest of his early childhood with Andrew, they had established their relationship despite Robin's family loss, throughout the years' Robin began learning army things he never learned previously at his old home.

2

King Martoon's return

During throughout the establishing bond with Robin and Andrew, Robin starts moving on within the fact his family no longer reaches to where he stands thereupon after King Martoon's attack, reality has come to a check alongside with a momentous massacre and a great many of lost dreams, therefore, It's unexplainable, after all, Robin's childhood days with his family no longer continues. A new insufferable era has changed the flow of what used to be a habitual norm, the new fate has arisen at once right after King Martoon's invasion struck the Earth, everyone from worldwide is aware of the fact that King Martoon exists!

Andrew reinstates his foster-living with Robin no matter what menacing challenger comes to pass such an underestimated facility. Things will be turn out to be more embellished than imagined, perhaps a convolution might prevail at some point, but, this juncture of complication could simply be a misjudgement or just a fallacy for the fact that human bonding brings altercation that deprives the sight of enlightenment upon the truths, we dip into a great depth that beholds this grievous epoch awaits a looming nearing towards Robin in a twinkling.

On the other hand, the intense innermost darkness concealed the connection of other possible outlandish realms as some scientists postulate out on the worldwide media here and now, King Martoon remains presumed scarcely evil for this time being. The Insatiable Majesty himself also holds a condemnation to meddling in other worlds in the past theoreticians preaches! These villains will not back down until they claim whatever they thirst for, during this era, galactic battles beyond human cognisance will go on to fight for a vigorous conquest!

Hours of darkness, in an ordinary mundane street, the winds were quite blustery at this time of the night. A sprinkling of houses down the street, there, a brick semi-detached home enclosed with birch wooden fences.

So, this was the time Robin sat quietly devouring his dinner at a small round table while Andrew sat opposing face to face with Robin, it occurs that they're having fried chicken with a side of potatoes and broccoli. They noshed their feast, subsequently, Andrew's phone went shuddering with vibration making an alarming din, Robin frightened with a jump abruptly!

Andrew laid a hold of his phone which was lying at the left-hand side of his dinner, he got the conversation going, Robin assumed anyway it could have been Andrew's pal.

"Yeah listen, I thought we agreed on the deal!" Andrew looked confusingly irritated, Robin paid no attention to listening to this conversation "we made a deal! Remember?" Andrew chastises the unrecognised incognito.

Thereafter a few ensuing minutes of the conversation, eventually, Andrew hung up his phone with a slam without any notice!

Andrew returns to pig out on his dinner, "to be honest son... Why do people have to be so egotistical and undiplomatic?" Andrew felt as if he's been deceived by the past rabble betrayal of diabolical living souls he once faithfully devoted as Andrew would have thought of anyway! Robin's dining ceased and he took one gaze at Andrew with a crystal-clear clarification, thought Robin to himself *"it's obvious these people don't give heed regarding the fact they come from rash families!"* as Robin is about done champing his dinner.

Afterward, they ingested the preponderance of their dinner, Robin carefully places his plate in the dishwasher. Afterwards, Robin went sprinting upstairs passing all the rooms, Robin's bedroom the furthermost part was at the bottom end of the hall. Robin sets his foot into his room while his door was wide opened.

He got his hands on his black dumbbells, it felt a little cumbersome weight, but, Robin was vigorously stout in his competence. Robin ensconced himself onto the bed and got started with his exercise.

A precipitous interruption by Andrew all of a sudden walks into Robin's room. "I'm gonna fasten down your window, It's a bit too chilly at night."

Andrew goes ahead to close the window, it hardly provoked Robin, Robin recommences hoisting his dumbbells! Shortly later on, Robin got drowsy after wrapping up his usual exercise routine, he de-junked his stuff away into his massive wardrobe, dressed into his banded pyjamas, and made his way into his bed with the cover to muffle him for the night. During the dead of night, lampposts in the street obfuscated by the closed windows and curtains, Robin slumbers fast asleep in the absence of light.

Hours of darkness swell, an unknown eccentric familiar squeaky sound shrieked out of nowhere, Robin roused from his bed in the middle of the night! Robin felt disturbed, but, he goes out his way to find his elucidation, he dallied around the room for clues that might justify the whole peculiar occurrence, he thought it would have been the foxes tittering near the outer forest, so, he turns to inspect outside his casement window.

Not a thing in sight that could have made such a sound, however, Robin won't capitulate within despair that easily, he was desirous to endeavour to find the secrets, he simply couldn't let it anguish more trauma, then, Robin started to realise about the squeaky sound. He thought that the sound must have been comparable to a coincidental random resonance in the past that he heard some long time ago that ultimately made him think back to, but, Robin couldn't seem to fully recollect at that occasion.

Then, Robin started to hear footsteps thumping from the hall outside his room, in an instant the door opened, It was just Andrew "Son, you're behind time, why are you still tossing and turning at this hour?"

Robin began to notice that Andrew was all anxious, he stood up with a dull calm face "what was that squeaky sound I heard, is someone stalking us?" at this point, Robin generally wanted to know while Andrew blew the subject quickly right out of the conversation.

"It's fine, don't get overwrought about it, please, a bit of shut-eye!" Robin got himself into bed once more, Andrew peeped outside the window, he scurried away out of Robin's room, Robin could hear Andrew's thumping downstairs.

Robin still wanted to discern the obscure sound, but, Andrew started to shout over the phone to some anonymous person. It was more than what Robin had bargained for, it only raised more questions for Robin's inquisitiveness.

Andrew persisted with his bellow on the phone, although, Robin was unclear of what Andrew was talking about or who he was talking too. He decided to snoop downstairs to find more of a sense upon the squeaky sound and Andrew's bizarre behaviour that Robin was worried about!

Robin tiptoed down each stair at a time, before he'd step his foot in the living room Robin decided to peep throughout the door to see, as Andrew plodded towards the hall, Robin toppled over onto the floor, Andrew heard Robin's sudden wallop, he rushed to the hallway, there. He saw Robin lying on the floor, he goes in his way to help Robin off the floor.

Andrew apologised, "Oops!! Sorry if I woke you up!" however, Andrew also started to notice Robin wasn't himself lately. "It's fine, but, I noticed that you're acting unusually."

Robin started to question his unsettling bother "I know! I haven't been myself a short time ago" Andrew was totally aware of flux.

Robin started to feel a sign of relieving Andrew that he's out of harm's way, Andrew smirked at Robin, Robin embraced Andrew with great fondness "I'd never have the affinity to someone if they weren't like you!"

Robin gave a bright look at Andrew, Andrew patted Robin on the head "get some shut-eye now son, do not let a thing fret to you!" Robin agreed to do so.

Robin ascended upstairs to his room, he approached the door to his room that was wide open. He goes back up onto his bed, he began his dozing throughout the rest of the night. The skies are murky, It's almost as if the sounds are inaudible, it's probable you can feel a soothing sensation of the wind outside.

Enclosed with an utter hush, an unforeseen thwack came out of nowhere, Robin didn't hearken at first, He continues to be in his beauty sleep, then, the startling pound happened twice, this time, Robin awakened from his bed with fright, he walks swiftly to the hall, Robin prowls downstairs, Robin assumed Andrew's asleep anyway.

The unremitting thumping continued to repeat itself, Robin ambles into the living room. He searches to give ear to the sound. It appears that the sound was coming from the basement, he was reluctant momentarily, but, it only is an ephemeral cursory, Robin felt eager and willing to enter to find out what the noise was coming from anyway. So he left the basement door ajar, he snatched a torch from the living room drawer, so, he scoured through the tenebrous basement, the mysterious noise had gotten strident as he got closer, it got to the point that the floor began to quiver, then, he headed to the washing machine to where the sound was heard, Robin opened the door seal, there, nothing was in sight!

Robin went back up to the living room, he was befuddled while he still explored around. The sound bursts again! Now, it was coming from the outer backyard, Robin patters into the kitchen, he still had the torch in his possession, he emerged outside the backyard, he sought vaguely up until Robin once more heard the sound coming near the gate to the front, the sound kept moving to different places as Robin arrived at every scene the sound came from.

He decided to go after the sound, he had his intent to ascertain the mystery. Robin bolted to the gate, then, he walked furtively outside the front of his house onto the walkway.

An adventitious holler that Robin gleans over in the distance, a rather inglorious man had appeared out of the blue. The shrouded man came closer to Robin, without warning, Andrew jostled his way out of the door, then grappled Robin with hefty vigour "get away from him you scoundrel!!!" Andrew started to go on full insensitively defensive against the unknown man.

Robin couldn't think clearly to the situation he just witnessed; Andrew looked offended against this uncanny figure. Andrew peered at Robin for a moment, then, he took Robin to his house at once.

After they got in the house, Robin dashed upstairs to his room, then, he looked out of his window, Robin noticed something suspicious about the anonymous figure, when Andrew turned away from the shadow, he would drag out a little gun out his pocket every time Andrew wasn't looking.

Robin was aghast, Andrew began to foot himself back to the house, however, the anonymous being began sneaking into the house through the backyard. He was enraged at this mysterious guy, Robin realized that Andrew knew right along the man wasn't just any wanton human.

Robin figured that if he watched the anonymous everywhere he goes, then, Robin would find out who this guy really is! Robin knew for a fact right away this is one way to protect Andrew.

Robin was about prepared to make his move out until he heard a thwack from upstairs, then, Robin saw Andrew in possession of the nameless man. "You scummy being!!!"

This filled Robin with indignation, he was at that point in the state of agitation, Andrew got shoved to the side, and the anonymous person proceeded towards Robin "All of the things you have lived through this aeon, I expected this day to arise!" this only raised more questions for Robin, but, he didn't care to ask.

Robin hared over to Andrew distraught, the anonymous gave them a sinister look with a knife at his hand, he was close to attack, but without warning, a red cloudy portal popped out of nowhere, what's even more surprising is the squeaky sound was coming from that portal!

King Martoon came out in a flash, Robin couldn't get around upon what has been beholden, King Martoon ignored everyone around him, Robin went after King Martoon as he made his way passed downstairs.

Andrew got back up on his feet distressed and began chasing after Robin!

King Martoon was heading outside the backyard, Robin stayed behind, Andrew emerged outside the backyard behind King Martoon. Andrew stood in front of the door opened, King Martoon cackled "you think you can just take high horse at this point, Andy, I don't imagine you dream it, pity!"

Andrew didn't back down to the insatiable majesty whilst the anonymous ran passed Robin on his way out of the back gate.

Robin went back into the kitchen, what Robin had just witnessed was a devastating thing to see Andrew drawing up a fight that he will never forget. He saw King Martoon grasp onto Andrew, King Martoon scowled at Robin with his menacing glowing eyes, it petrified Robin to his core, before Robin could say anything, he fainted onto the floor!

Everything was filled with pure darkness, he will have thought until his eyes start to rise again with raised questions that will be awaited in the fate of Robin. King Martoon strikes again with dominance in his pride, his worst shipping progenitors have served their majesty lasting enduring times.

3

The Escape from the Army

It's been scandalous since the execrable arrival, Andrew's tenderness went evanescent cannot go forgotten by The Insatiable Majesty, this incandescent happening has triggered Robin's stubbornness by the blemish deaths of the family who once been sticking to his side for years, even if they fought by a simple misapprehension.

This warm sanguine feeling Robin discerns withstands any path he'll encounter known to the monkey, he shall make his break free anytime, sooner or later will perceive his glimpse of the obscure dimension of who King Martoon really transpires to be, the villain of Robin's nightmares that comes by every so often.

This new beginning depends on what kind of fierce comes into Robin's path of the unknown conspiratorial contenders that will eventually locus together when it comes to square up to, to confront and face new sources of dangerous foes. on the other hand, Robin becomes a dauntless insight at this point of his life!

September 7th, 2014
(USA Annapolis Maryland – Army training centre)
Robin is determined to change the world someday by becoming the vice-president. Unfortunately for him, his dream is been shattered by his contemporary General, a leader named Tam Sheridan, the General is rather pompous, strict and extremely rude from his solid belt to his sturdy and powerful voice which roars out a thundering echo all across the departments and hallways can be full-throated. Robin is currently working as head chef in a cafeteria at the military training station, he works in a large kitchen station with other chefs on board. Throughout his entire career of military training, he meets Steven which would consider Robin and him to be best roommates within their compassion withstands all friendships Robin's been through.

One night, Robin is just about to complete his shift, as usual, he cleans up and gets his stuff good to go. After he finished his dinner service, he walked at one of the exit doors to have a smoke outside. Robin goes outside with his cigarette in his right hand and sits down onto a stair slab in front of the building at the back ally with all the aircraft and planes standing about, Robin begins smoking for ten minutes, he sits around thinking about when he'll ever get the chance to be nominated to take leadership and find King Martoon for good, for all those years ever since he took away both side of all his family.

After Robin finished smoking, he dumped it in the bin and walked back inside the building through the same exit he previously been out of, he walked down to his room, when Robin entered his room, he is slightly exhausted through all that work, he felt like he was about to dose.

Robin got dressed into his pyjamas, he tucked himself into bed and laid his head onto the velvety pillow with a smooth duvet bed cover. Suddenly, the door opened who revealed to be

Robin's roommate Steven "How's your shift tonight Sergeant Monkey?" asked Steven "It's a total drag! I had to control two stations because a few of my junior chefs were sick!" replied Robin.

"Wish to be at liberty if you get nominated huh?" Steven mentioned with a sarcastic happy tone.

"I'm getting sick and tired of it, I wanted this nomination so bad! Nine rejections I had to go through ever since I joined at fifteen!" grimaced Robin with hatred!

"Maybe we should give it a wrap shall we?" asked Steven.

Robin turned at the window beside his bed, he sighed "Yeah! let's just get this night over with!!" Robin answered.

Steven climbed up onto the top bunk bed and Robin slept down the bottom bunk bed, they fell asleep after everyone finished their duty.

September 8th, 2014
(USA Annapolis Maryland – Army training centre)
The next morning, Robin woke up abruptly, heard a pound from their door.

"Hey!! what was that for Darren?!" shouted Steven, Robin looked up from his bottom bunk bed at Steven with bags under his eyes, he rubbed his eyes, got out of bed and then he got changed into his uniform for the nomination assembly that was due to begin.

"May as well get prepared or else Tam will thrash us like usual!" asserted Robin.

"I'll do that! Just keep him out of my sight!!" grinned Steven with his miniature, robust, sweaty fists strapping together.

Then they got ready and packed their stuff for the nomination until Robin heard Tam Sheridan roaring through the corridors whilst the walls quivered rapidly, "Crud! Better be fast!" he demanded. Robin and Steven agreed to do so!

Robin walked out of his room along with Steven strolling through their section department, Steven put his head down, Robin felt slightly concerned, so, he asked Steven, "What's upsetting you brother?"

"You're not going to get it Robin?" weirdly replied Steven. he scratched his forehead with his right hand, Robin shrugged the thought off his mind "I guess this is an obvious stress pain you faced since last time you took those..."

Steven interrupts Robin with a stomp "I know you're not going to be nominated! Whatever you do, don't think you're gonna get nominated anytime soon pal!" Then Robin got bemused by him with bewilderment.

Steven halted with a straight dull emotion, Robin also stopped and looked to Steven again! "Why are you acting like some foreseeable soothsayer!? Gee, you become some darn weirdo!" Robin opined.

Steven didn't say another word and went on his way to the assembly hall, Robin watched Steven as he continues to saunter passed all the corridors, Robin followed Steven on the way.

They continued walking, but didn't make any eye contact after the awkward moment. Robin turned around to see everyone else behind heading towards assembly.

The pair arrived in the hall, they sat down onto a dining bench, in a moment of prattling from everyone else, a group of people a few tables away talking on rumours, talking behind Tam's back and Robin overhears their gossip. Steven chuckled a slight, meanwhile Tam marched through the door.

"Attention!!!" screamed Tam.

The nomination assembly began, everyone listened in on Tam to hear who he's going to nominate this year. Tam looked at

Robin, who saw Tam looking at him. *Here we go again!"* thought Robin.

"Hey!! Sergeant Monkey!!!" snarled Tam.

Robin remained calm.

Tam continued, "You're early! Wow, you are so desperate for this moment!"

Steven checked his watch, Robin became speechless for a couple of seconds.

"Hold up! I thought you'd be expecting us by now!" said Steven with confusion.

Everyone else stared at Tam. "I knew you wouldn't get a beating from me, unlike last time!!" chortled Tam with a grin in his smirk.

"So, we came early for nothing!" questioned Steven feeling miffed.

Robin couldn't believe what he had just discovered. Afterward, Steven stood up from his seat, he pointed at Tam, shaking wildly and was just about to turn into an infuriated assaulter towards everyone else.

Robin eventually yanked Steven back onto his seat.

"Anyway, the reason I brought you here earlier than I should is that little Toby had been insubordinate with the standard guidelines in this centre, he's today been charged with theft and vocal abusing!" Tam explained. "you will not underestimate us in any circumstances, do you understand!" he declared.

Everyone concurred, Robin and Steven saluted in agreement.

Tam raised his left hand up "every life counts to keep our people safe from intruders that'll try to invade our territory, creatures from an enigmatic domain, it's about time we shall nominate our soldiers for departure.

Robin begins to sweat as Tam pulls out the official list. Everyone jumped up for hope and gleeful joy, Steven watched Robin's reaction it is dumbfounded agitating!

Tam called out other names as Robin continued to sweat more gradually.

"Calm down sergeant monkey!" said Steven.

"I've been dreaming to get the heck out of this prison cell for years, I can't wait to show that King Martoon whose side he's been messing with all this time in my life!!" said Robin.

Tam is just about to call the last name. "And now, our only remaining nominee for this year is gonna be..." the suspenseful reveal is about to be called out.

Robin glanced at Tam "David Herd!!!" proclaimed Tam. "Nominees! file up in a line!!" Tam gives the order and the nominees march behind where Tam was standing.

Robin's crestfallen defeat comes by Steven's sympathy triggered at this moment of despair, Robin couldn't break off grasping his fist. "I've been working for the last ten years in the military, still to this day Tam refuses to designate me!!!" Robin desisted for a minute.

Steven watched Tam as he walks with the nominees to the backyard, then, Steven turns to face Robin, he sees the vexation coming from the outside of Robin's expression. "You're upright and honest. The general just pretends to be a great chief but really he's just an upside-down kingpin."

Robin muttered, then Stephen walked off disgruntled at a loss of words.

Robin got off his seat, and goes to string along with everyone else going back to the main corridor. He felt lousy and turned down undeservedly. As he continued trudging through the hallway, he accidentally bumped into Steven's bully.

"Hey!! aren't you that Sergeant monkey?" as if Robin's getting cross-examined from the mutual bully. "Hey Darren, I heard you satirising me the other day. Steven told me as well as I am the only monkey who's around!" acknowledged Robin, they keep walking on with a conversation going.

Darren looked at Robin into his eyes, Robin ceased with a halt suddenly. "Look pal!! if you want to fight with me? You can tell it to Tam!! I'm not in the mood for fights!!" grumbled Robin.

Darren is about to thwack Robin in the face, he looks suspiciously dubious, Robin immediately makes fleet for it, Darren didn't dare to seize over at him, so, he just strolled off.

Robin continued walking, he sees his room plate, he enters his room, still clenching his fists more violent, he growled loudly and slammed the door behind him. He turned his anger from Darren back to Tam. "Barbarous scumbag!!! Why the heck doesn't he just nominate me, and I'll somehow get my idea on defeating King Martoon once and for all!".

He sat down on a sofa chair in his room, he gawked at the wall for several minutes anguished, then, slams his hands onto the armrest cushion. He slowly begins scratching the arm cushions intensively, his hands are already beginning to turn red as if any boiling kettle would. He couldn't resist the pain of rejection anymore, he draws a knife from his pocket and rapidly stabbing it into his training dummy at the corner of his room, Robin is miserable and crabby for the rest of the evening.

At midnight, Robin still sits in his room looking out the window, outside he sees a dull sky and watched the rain pouring from the grey clouds above. HE still feels snappish about the rejection he'd been given to himself, his eyes were red, his face is blue, Robin felt like rubbish at this moment of time. he begins to have short suicidal thoughts, Robin couldn't deny that all the negativity that goes on in his head is undeniably bonkers.

Steven knocked the door, but Robin ignores what's around him. Steven slowly opened the door, Robin didn't seem to care.

"Sorry you didn't get the nomination." said Steven.

"If you feed me that word nomination into my throat once more! I will slaughter this dummy apart with this army syringe knife!" intimated Robin full of anxiety.

Steven understands Robin's exasperation.

Robin breathes in and out again and again for three minutes.

"You should probably get ready for preparation for tomorrow!" mentioned Steven, but at the same time, he feels sorrowful for Robin's tenth rejection. Steven's expression is unbearable

Robin forcefully agrees to Steven's objective, he puts the knife into his bag, he gets dressed into his chef clothing. When he was ready he tramped outside his. He closes the door, goes through the corridor past the other doors, the lights are faint, Robin generally felt careless at this point!

He went into the dining hall and sees the door into the kitchen, as soon as he sets his foot right in, the other workers welcomed him.

"Sir! since you were gone, we decided to prepare all the work for you, Take a break mate, you earned it!!" one of the junior chefs said with an admirable salute which cheered Robin a little bit. Robin winked at his workers, then, Robin went over to his office next door from the kitchen, he entered and sits down with a banana. Alongside, his desk had a note attached to the front of the basket. Robin shifted the basket to the left edge beside his computer. Suddenly, Robin starts banging his head onto the surface of his keyboard, as he smacks his head onto the keyboard, you could almost hear the sound of the most absurd and riotous type thumping, he keeps doing it for several minutes, he still couldn't hold back against the rejection.

Meanwhile, Steven approaches the kitchen door, Steven knocked on the door.

"Robin!!! We need to talk!!!" Steven calls from outside.

Robin calls a halt and goes outside the kitchen into the dining area. There, he sees Steven sitting at one of the table benches at the front of the cafeteria.

"We need to discuss an important matter in your hands!". Robin and Steven both begin conversing "It's about that nomination, I found out that Tam first thought to nominate you at the beginning, but, he quickly changed to his alternative nominee, it's simply the fact he doesn't see you as a fit as a solver of wisdom."

Steven claimed that Tam is allegedly hiding some kind of secret evidence from Robin.

Robin's eyes open wide appalled "Are you being genuine here! He thinks I, Sergeant Monkey don't have all that power to stand out in the crowd!!! That's disreputable!!!" mumbled Robin with his teeth clenched together. He felt stabbed in the back for a good amount of long-lasting decades. "That's it!!! tomorrow I'm writing a complaint about this!!!" yelled Robin.

He stumbled away, down through the main corridor hall. Steven quickly follows behind as Robin goes in a ruffle stomping down the corridors, Robin still feeling indignant. Steven remained cool for the rest of tonight.

Steven doesn't even try to get under Robin's skin any further, instead, he lets Robin blow off his steam. Robin immediately lay back onto his bunk bed, Steven climbed up onto his top bunk, where he sinks into his soft mattress. they tucked themselves into the duvet covers and they waited until next morning whilst the barely audible sounds of murmuring crickets stridulating far away under natures hidden mysteries we cannot explain.

*

The following sunless morning, Robin awoke from his bunk bed, turned to gaze outside his window. He saw the dark plum clouds hovering across the skies with the sun ill illuminating by the gloomy mist above. He turns over to look at his room door before sitting up to put his leg out of his bed. He stood up and headed to the drawer to change into his casual army clothes. He pulled his boots on, next, he approached the door and opens it. He goes in for a quick shower in the bathroom before breakfast service.

On the spur of the moment, Robin comes to a standstill for a minute, he continuously has thoughts about those ten declined nominations, he starts to think about Tam's behaviour towards him and the fact that he Robin is a monkey and everyone else just constrains him and also generally torments him.

Robin takes a dekko at the time on his digital watch, he realised that it was far too soon to begin his service right now. All the other rooms were silent as Robin presumed everyone would be snoozing at this time anyway. However, Robin knew that Tam usually woke up before nine! Robin comes up with a scheming idea, but, he'd need answers from Steven before he gets to the bottom of this, he returned to his room. He went over to Steven's top bunk, Robin reached his hand over to Steven's bed cover and jerked it right off Steven's arms "Steven! We need to talk," Robin whispered into Steven's ear. Robin juddered Steven's left leg with mild movement "Please! I need answers from you!", Robin keeps clutching onto Steven's leg.

Steven stirred slowly, he rose from his bed and takes a peep at Robin. "What is the issue? Something to do with Tam Sheridan again?" questioned Steven accompanied by his incertitude.

Robin clambered onto the top bunk bed, he pointed his index finger directly up at the ceiling. "Exactly Steven!! Tam is the main suspect here and the focus of our intentions!" a response with such candid recognition.

"Are you still groaning about the rejection of the assembly nomination?" questioned Steven. They stay sitting up and discuss Tam Sheridan.

At an instant after such a long conversation, Robin climbed down from Steven's bed with impetuous haste. He grabbed a piece of paper with a map view diagram of the army training centre.

Steven goggles at the map "you're planning to escape! aren't you?" Steven asked in an anxious matter.

Robin took a step back for a moment slightly surprised. Steven rolled his eyes with an obvious concern, then climbed down there. He moves towards Robin, and attempted to seize and pinch the map.

"Steven!!! This is the key to our escape, I don't have any other options!!" shouted Robin.

Steven, however, looked away from Robin. His caution only made him willing to discard the map into the recycling bin.

Robin clenched his fists together once more; he stormed over to Steven. "Do you really want to draw your breath to the rest of this torture with a damn unacquainted man who bosses you around!!?" Robin wanted a sincere honest answer. He doesn't feel the same way as he used to, he used to look up to Steven.

Steven turned to face Robin again, placed his hands onto Robins shoulders. "Mate! this is desertion!! you're about to commit a nauseating offence!!" Steven bellowed out beyond his cool stance.

Robin gave a black look to Steven. Steven noticed a slip of teensy tears from his friend. He begins imploring Robin not throw his life away under the sovereignty of King Martoon.

Robin couldn't comprehend the reasoning behind Steven's words. It would necessitate the end of Robin's desire to become the one who put a kibosh to King Martoon's dreadful reign.

Steven has these mixed thoughts flowing inside his mind about Robin's struggle pain upon everything. Suddenly, they start to become aware of the whole picture, Robin glimpses at Steven with a solicitous smile. His friend smirks as well and lays his hand on Robin's left shoulder. They come to their senses of the reality, then. Steven gets a sense of empathy towards Robin's painful journey.

Robin tramps out the room and sprints across the main corridor. When he arrived at Tam's office, he first knocks the door. There is no response from the other side of the door. He thumped the door again but harder. Still nothing. He is irritated into a slight huff, so, what he did next is vile, he slams the door forcefully, as luck would have it, the door didn't burst and divide into chunks of wood pieces.

Sheridan appeared. At first and foremost, the General goes fume at Robin for a deliberate near destroying to his bronze shiny polished door. "What in the name of bullets was that for Sergeant monkey!!!?" interrogated Tam within close to his boiling point.

"Tam, I have to address an accusation against your actions towards making me and my squaddies imposed!" Robin said in disillusion.

"I need to stop you right there!! You do know that everyone in this has to follow all my rules, it's obligatory in order to protect America!" Tam responds with an informal tone.

However, it's obvious to Robin what he sees in Tam's crabby red eyes. He still didn't find this whole thing acceptable. Straight away, he struck his fist down onto Tam's desk! "I'm not complaining about the rules, it's you. You're the one who takes no notice of me when every single year at the nomination, regardless of the fact that I'm a monkey, you still don't consider me!!"

Sheridan leered at Robin with disgust. He hauled his chair forward close to the edge of the desk, Tam gawked into Robin's eyes, then, he puts his hand gently onto his desk "Face it, Sergeant monkey, if you want to succeed in..."

Robin interrupted Tam by slamming his other fist onto the desk.

Tam jumped from his seat with instant disapproval

"This excuse isn't going to work on me as it always did Tam!!!" wailed Robin with a raging powerful voice.

"Can't you see the kind of rogue you are contrasted to King Martoon!!!"

They continued to argue.

Steven abruptly appears in front of Tam's office, he looks appalled.

"Robin!! I don't approve of this!!!" Steven feels more alarmed as Tam stares at him momentarily whilst Robin couldn't sustain the current situation that he put himself into.

Tam now feels betrayed with immense amounts of anger inside of him!

Steven grabs Robin from Tam's office "Are you insane?" whispers Steven aggressively.

Robin down at the floor "I gotta do what I need to do, for me!" replied deeply Robin.

He thinks the unthinkable, of all those times that he was ready for his venture.

Steven begins to have thoughts that are beyond description, and the fact that Robin's dedication is for the most part wanting to escape the centre in order to strive his adventure to the next level instead of playing the waiting game.

Tam tramps outside his office downright offended at both Robin and Steven. He sees them beside his door leaning against the wall to the right. "You're out of order Sergeant monkey! Useless piece of blarney that you are!!!" hissed Tam.

 Robin had no time for drama in this case of him crying for freedom.

Tam then walks back into his office disgruntled as usual in a daily basis.

As Steven watches Tam stumble away, Robin sits down onto the floor with a cigarette and a lighter in both his hands.

"Schmuck! He sure is gullible, here, this is the chance to beat a hasty retreat from this place!" urged Robin with a slim smirk, Steven looked disgusted at Robin for a minute, but, he gets the insight of Robin's understanding quickly again.

Steven is totally aware of this crime more than just delinquency; Robin begins to think back to the map plan that Steven trashed in the recycling bin!

Robin urges Steven to bear with his plan, then, he looked up at his friend, Steven starts to feel peer pressure inside his thoughts. So, both Robin and Steven ran past the left corridor to the main, after, they sneak across every room with a bunch of surveillance spy cameras surrounding in the main department section, Steven starts to think that Robin could be ethical after all.

Robin runs into the room snatches the map plan out of the recycling bin, Steven starts to question Robin on how they are going to get King Martoon "I heard about evidence over at Britain, that's we're heading!" declared Robin with pride and determination! Steven's anxiety begins to diminish over time gradually. They both are beginning to put the plan into action.

Robin shut the door, and laid out the map onto the table, Steven glanced at the map. He gets overwhelmed with befuddlement; Robin starts to conduct his way into the plan. "Right! we're going to divert the guards out of our breakout exit."

As Robin sets his plan into action, Steven hastily implores his suggestion with his other alternative "Or, how about we make our haste on splitting up, basically I will be the decoy and you make the run!" Robin was pleased with Steven's preferable ploy, and agrees to the change of the plan "I guess we can stick with your plan of action! This is the one chance we have or else we're dead and buried!!" The final piece of the plan is to meet outside the back alley once they are out of harm's way.

Before they could make headway, they hear footsteps outside their room. Robin said "Shucks, we need to do this quite a brisk, but, just don't behave too fishy!"

They tacitly began to sneak out of their door, they knew there were four guards patrolling through the hall that Steven rushes to silence whilst Robin slinks his way to the back alley exit.

He gets underway passing from end to end of each corridor, Robin finally catches the sight of the back exit and emerges outside the military back alley.

Steven having successfully lost the guards turns up out of the blue. "I'll draw up the engine, get on mate" as Steven quickly clambers onto the plane and starts the engine.

Robin also climbs aboard, Robin fastens his seat belt, the engine starts to kick off, it makes a tumultuous deafening racket.

The aircraft plane starts to take wing, but, without warning Tam dashes out to only see Robin's immense abscond retreat had been the greatest moments there to betide. However, this moment is also been a double-dealing perfidy for Tam, Robin guffaws at Tam standing with wrath. "Escapes can be empathy after you rub someone the wrong way, best of luck upon your trail!!!"

Robin enjoyed this moment more than he ever could in his life after all the things he had been tormented throughout the depths of spurn, Steven pulls the lever causing the aircraft to soar off to the skies!

Tam boils with his mighty fume. "When I haul in you and Steven, you'll be remorseful of what you've done!!!" Tam sends the scouts to chase down Robin and Steven, so, they do hop onto their aircraft.

All scouts start chasing after them as they took off to the skies! Robin and Steven kept up their journey heading to make way to Britain on what they have to offer touching on King Martoon's existence.

In a trice upon still of dawn is just about to undertake gushes of fulsome wind, up in the alloy inky clouds swarming across each other in front of their twilight sunlight!

Robin stands by to see his new awaiting baffling voyage. "We did it I knew this would work out more than I expected!" as Robin ventures with strive beyond the sea on which he and Steven hustle over the ocean, but, titchy hazel stones piddle down showering into the waters.

"Listen I only did this for you because Tam Sheridan thinks that he can just slave us around like that!" Steven starts to feel solicitous within his enduring friendship, but, he abashes his felony!

Robin yawned and lay back with his arms placed at the back of his head, Steven looked out for any scout troopers who might try to track them down.

"I wonder if the rumour is true?" Steven wants to know if they'll ever find King Martoon, but Robin on the other hand has it all in his game plan.

"If it's not, perhaps, It'll come to us by and by!" Robin feels unruffled and perhaps he enervates the drowsiest fatigue.

It was many hours into the flight, Robin heavily sat up from his seat. He saw Steven who seems to zero in on his piloting, and they begin flying over Ireland.

Robin suddenly hears planes at the far side of their path. Out of the blue, Robin could see hurling bullets whizz, then, Robin knew that the scouts had caught up to them.

Robin alarms Steven, and they go into dismay! "How on earth did they find us!?" whined Steven.

Robin rattles along with his plan to fly his way out of this mess "Don't bother about it, Steven! let's go on full sonic speed!!!" Robin isn't having any of it.

Steven heaved the lever onto turbo, while the scouts stick their eyes on the two deserters. Then, suddenly, Robin and Steven come across an aeroplane. Robin and Steven still kept insight of any scouts, they know what they're in for at this moment during their greatest bolt for freedom to Britain. Robin could not have been more grateful than how far he had come.

Things became completely silent for a moment, they continue to fly across the northern waters, Robin could see they're passing Ireland, the murkiness made it difficult for them to see through!

All at once, those wily scouts caught up again!

Robin once again enraged said, "Steven, those chamchas are back on our tail again, go turbo again!!" even so Steven turns the lever a second time, the worst luck happens, the lever snaps right off just as soon he pushes it forward. Steven's anxiety only swells at this point, they think now that they are doomed! He looks over at Robin with sweat flowing. "Robin, we're toasted for good this time!"

Robin then notices that they are out of gas as well, therefore, their solution becomes even luckless!

This is when everything goes wild! Steven feels the fear of dread while the meltdown fills inside of Robin's constraint, then, Steven had enough. He pulls out a pistol that he loaded after he exposes himself with the pistol, he then points it directly to where his heart is before he could pull the trigger, Robin cuffs the pistol right off his hand making it fall down into the sea!

"Bro, don't do something that foolish! We have many things to fight for rather than just end your life here in the middle of a mayday!!!"

Robin heartens Steven with little eagerness. Robin chooses to take full control of driving instead. "Steven, let me charge control! I need to fix what I've gotten us into!!", so, they switched seats while they unstrapped their seat belts and they quickly moved seats. The scouts prepared to attack, of course.

Robin spotted their signal, and commenced dodging every attack feasible! He realised that there was a ginormous typhoon on their horizon.

The whole flight chase begins to get ridiculous. After all the pressure, Robin suddenly thinks up this rough idea he had in his mind that might work out.

"Right! We have no choice but to jump off when I drop, you drop, got it!?" He unfastened his seat belt, then, he pulled himself along towards the storage box at the back of the plane. He grabs two parachutes. "We're landing! Say goodbye to our night terrors and hello game changer!!" Robin chuckles with a grateful smile.

Robin puts the parachute on his back and gives Steven the other parachute. When they were ready Robin unlatched the door as fast as he could, jumped out of the plane with all speed. Steven had no other course of action but to pin his hope on seeking another day counting his existence, so, Steven grabbed his parachute and quickly strapped it onto his back while the scouts continue to follow the plane.

Steven madly jumps, falling down from the foggy skies, the plane began to drop down as well, but, just as it is falling, one of the scouts gets caught up and ripped the wings of the plane right off at the double. The battle only got more uttermost fierce.

Steven continues to dive through the fog clouds until he caught up with Robin "Son of a Jammy!!! It's getting feisty here Steven!" Robin utters his whammy awe.

Eventually, the scouts finally lost them! So, they split up and they drift into the mist to go hunt for them. Robin and Steven activate their parachutes, they swayed side by side Steven.

Robin clasped Steven on his shoulder, they continued to descend from the thunderous clouds. Spurts of heavy wind begin to blow. "Crud! Gods getting angry now, don't you think?" Steven feels the powerful force blowing through him, however, the wind puffs so mighty that Robin straight off feels his hand slipping away from Steven, so there, Robin tries to hold on as long as he can, but unfortunately, Robin couldn't withstand the turbulence any longer.

The mighty wind gets blustery stormy, before you know it, Robin slipped away from Steven and they take one last look at each other before they fade away into dark mist. Robin still feels the raining hale stones, but, it showers down fast, suddenly, a bunch of tiny hale stone pokes inside of Robin's eyes causing him to be sightless. Furthermore, it gets even rougher, Robin's parachute rips apart causing him to fall at peril! Therefore, Robin screams for his mortality.

Will Robin survive this chasmic fall to continue his pursuit of King Martoon alone? Will Robin ever get the odds of reuniting with Steven another time? Will Robin ever flee from Tam Sheridan to pursue his destiny conclusively? I do happen to know, but, I'll let you see for yourself!

The End?

The Flight of the Ladybird

Emma Taylor

Goodbye

I'm writing this to tell you I'm leaving.
Don't go looking for me to make sure I'm breathing.
I wasn't, but I think I can now.
I've never asked nor wanted for much,
I'll ever so dearly miss your sentiment and touch,
Though I beg of you for peace

Time has been exhausted for the body which I lived on lease.

I gathered some resources for my journey.
I won't need oxygen nor gravity
Though I leave behind the weight of the insufferable insanity.
I carry my soul and jigsaw memory.

Peace – in an untouched world.

This is goodbye though this is not where

I end.

Mercury

Nother mother resides on the grounds closest to the sun.
The irony
She always seemed to be connected to the star,
A way with the light and giving lost souls a direction.
But it burns.
The jurisdiction of Earth is in her hands.

whom did not require to be revolved around?

Mercury holds the lost messages of life.
Messages which gift you with a subtle visit
Need you notice their presence.
Mines was a ladybird, in the comfort of my bedroom on the
cold nights of December,
That night in December, funnily enough
It's a sign.

Not all are benevolent.
Who is?
I was always superstitious,
A bit of a dozy cow really...
Gullible.
Inclined to take what you want, as you do.
Melancholy mind games or fulfilling fate.
Nonetheless,
you noticed.

I am not afraid of dying
I am afraid

Of growing old
It isn't fair, is it?
Had I just a few more years, your memory in-tact and not
having to accept the fact that
It will always be too late.
You reached past me for whatever you saw
She seen something, we seen nothing but the hospital walls
And just like that,
Shes gone.
I would give you my favourite paint brush and we can cover
the grey areas
Which dimension has the Dementia got you in right now?
Perhaps we could paint you a way out.
My name is Emma, no I'm not the waitress. I'm Lynne's
daughter
I'm pleased to make your acquaintance Emma, you are a
beautiful girl.
~~I love you, Gran~~   Thank you, ma'am

I feel you with me, all of the time
And I have a feeling it's your fault that I failed every attempt I
tried to end it all
Thank you for that, by the way
She left for mercury many moons ago
I hope you got your memories back, but that
I'll never know.

Venus

Everything is pure,
The atmosphere here sings a peaceful tone to my ear,
I can smell home with my eyes.
Love, as I knew it.
I gently penetrate the surface as I land,
With only her permission.
Platonic plants strangle my ankles.
Vicious vines tear through the blanket of my bones
"Where are you taki-

....

Blood

Mine?
I struggle to stand in this wasteland.
My lips part to scream,

I have no voice

My skin is dissolving where I don't recall being touched.

Adulterate fucking fate.
....
And so, the healing begins.
Apparently, I can save this planet if I plant new seeds,
But nothing seems to grow.
It was my fault
It was my fault

It was my fault
It was my fault
It was my fault
One simply cannot cover old with new,
And I only have my shaky hands to dig.

Plant
The
Seeds
Deeper

How can it haunt my dreams if I didn't see a f-DON'T fucking
touch me!
Oh.. it was ... nothing.
Nobody will want me now, covered in spoiled spilled milk.
Is that.. is that milk?
Bitter tart, bastard.
The good news is, it doesn't hurt anymore,

It's just numb.

The hyper sex drive

Nobody ever told me about the forth coming
The hyper sex drive
And sleeping with strangers to make yourself feel alive
Maybe it'll balance it out
You know, the higher the body count we can block the non
consensual out
But since she's easy she's probably got diseases

Take it from experience, it doesn't fix the curse
Laying on your back wishing he just stole something
sentimental out your purse

With each grunt, a greater grudge against men

Robbed

Of my dignity,

if everything happens for a reason and my rapist is still
breathing, now he's a lawyer

To cover up for the brawl of the boys without baws who's
fathers must've taught them to get what they want,
women are toys

My blood on the walls, internal bleeding and broken ribs for
the slut with the slit between her hips where you believe your
party piece won't fit

It's too big

Not your fucking cock you selfish prick, aren't we supposed to
be wet for that shit?

Maybe it's women for me
No Emma that's selfish, you need to pick a team
Why is it I can't live my life in peace without being impaled
with a vampires teeth

It's for the attention, are you fucking kidding me?

The girls are giving me grief, they accept me but won't have a
sleepover anymore since sharing the same bed is suddenly strange

As if you think I'm from the same breed and really that deranged

Don't shower, brush your teeth, don't change clothes

Are you sure that's the outfit you were wearing?
it's not very exposed

I know you don't remember but how did the story go?

It's his word against mine
Apparently he didn't realise it was a crime and
We know there's date rape in your blood
He seems like a clever boy so I'm sure it's all a bit of a mix up

But she was probably asking for it mind,

I'm terribly sorry officer for wasting police time.

Earth, from afar

When you stand from afar
Earth is a marble of everything you've ever known,
compressed into a ball.

Air is disintegrating into crumbs, maybe that's
why we've been suffocating.
Realizing the crystal ball of fortune is the one
in which we reside
Everything we fear, stress and love is inside

Fire gone wild is to blame for the loss of
arches of trees, the wildlife and bees
As if we weren't doing that ourselves, forgive me, please
Ignite the poor behind closed doors
Live by the rules of the rich if you don't want starving kids
I don't know about you but I don't recall
mother nature teaching us this
Not that we've ever listened
Greed is one if our planet bides by survival of the richest.

Out with the ashes of material wealth lie the
glass hearts of the kind souls
Under oath that kindness can heal the world, rightfully so
Repercussions of earlier generations and the audacity to dream
of equality

Water covers 71% of the planet and money covers the rest
Oh, that explains the starvation and dehydration death rate
Rest assured, all our actions are pure, unless
Lies withhold the hope for a cure
Doomed, is the planet with only hope to improve.

The presence of absence

When is the last time you seen a ladybird?

When I was a kid they were on the paths, flowers and plants
I would collect them in my fathers empty cigarette packet with
a little bit of grass
I took them to my grandfather's grave forever to stay
I was only 6 but I remember that day.

I am only 23, why the fuck is there no leaves on the trees?
If for whatever reason its part of my story to have kids
They probably wont even know they exist

I've got a ladybird on my wrist, and I don't what it
to become a myth

Presence of positive spirit and symbolic of new beginnings
I am trying to use my initiative, but I don't think there are
many new beginnings to be had

Those were the days, I still had my fathers hand.

Mars

Mars is the home of mothers who never got to be.
The air is sweet
It is easy to breathe

I rode Opportunity
Navigation in an unknown location.

We endured great maroon sand dunes
To the top
A clear landscape of her war wounds.

A sandstorm will inevitably be her fate.
Not a single soul on the planet to pick her up.

"My battery is low and it is getting dark"
We failed her, from far far away
Maternal appetite to liquid legacy.

There may not be mothers,
But there is certainly life on Mars.

A delusion in evolution and malfunctioning machines.
Though I'm told technology can replenish you at the seams.

Jupiter

Leaping along the many moons,
I spoke with the gods before I spoke with the king.
Some warned danger,
Some encouraged pleasure.

It was my decision.

Caught in the current of the blurry white lines,
The clouds are not so pure.
The metallic flavoured fields of gas flash and flare.

It feels   i n   c   r   e   d   i   b   l   e

The melody of this weather will become a familiar pleasure.

A black hole has formed in my pupil,
Sucking in my own life.

Supreme dopamine

Rot.

The king has a punishment in mind.
Banished and destroyed in the great spot of reddish rouge hell.

None of the moons warned me of the aftermath.
Somethings must be self-taught.
Also,
I think I left my jaw on Jupiter?

I step back into the beautiful colours and promises of happiness
A gravitational pull is undefeatable
And I choose to never do it again.

Saturn

She's a big girl,
But she's lovely.

One size ~~never~~ fits all,
You say ring, I say crown
Either way, she wears it well
She's killing it

She's complicated
Confused

She's trying to figure out how a size, let alone,
A number
doesn't define her when they add unnecessary horror words
like
'plus'
'extra, extra, extra large'

I'll give you fucking extra-

She can simultaneously fit two sizes of clothing and wearing
shoes from the kids section,
Now that's just unfair,

So here's the thing;
nobody else actually cares,
they wont say a word ~~to you~~,
they wouldn't dare.
If they love you,

They love you are you are.
It is possible to love someone else and not yet love yourself,
They will teach you how to

Then why can I not simply stand in front of a mirror and
admire for once?

Progress is slow,
It doesn't need to start with a diet and exercise

It can start with eating the things that make you happy,
Wearing what makes you feel good, not to fit in

Not to be fat or thin

And definitely not to blend in.

Uranus

I find no comfort.
Shivering and searching for any resources to
Function.
Most would manage fine.
This is not the harsh reality that I have hoped for.
Careless and helpless

My independence was wasted.

Misfortune.

She provides what she can for all,
A place of protection and unjudged.
Acceptance in return.
This isn't adequate for some.

Her one rule is that nobody rules her land.
But rules come with controversy, don't they?
It wasn't your intension?
My ass

Nothing grows on these trees.

My mistake.

I was warned everything would be frozen.
Colder and more alone than I've ever known.

I forced shards of broken glass down my throat to wash down
the words

"I told you so".

I swallow shards of glass and my pride.
Despite my bleeding gullet, I preferred the glass.

Blood is supposed to be thicker than water but it's easy to
swallow
you can pick your family if they don't pick you,
I promise you a happier life with the ability to choose.
Friends, all the same in a two-player game
They should be the ones to pick you up on the bad days and
protect you from shame
Family and friends are supposed to be two different things,
In my eyes, they're all just the same.

Family doesn't mean for money in birthday cards,
It's a nice gesture but I would've rather you were there for my
parents' night and the shitty report cards.

Neptune

I put the 'I' in irrational
Everything is steady
Everything is calm,
Everything is going okay,
And I'm actually feeling pretty happy for once.
Everything remains steady, like a statue
It doesn't match the crumbling, devastating sights in my mind
It just.. stands
still
I must think over ~~and over and over and over and over and over and over~~ all of the things I have said or done which could
be miss conceived,
the times I've portrayed no other than greed.

My heart is the seed
My brain is a sunflower
The petals will already be plucked before they are fully grown
he love me, ~~he loves me not, he loves me, he loves me not, he loves me, he loves me~~... not
Though where flowers grow, the crop does not rot.
Vitamin C for the seed and water for me.
Except I won't grow anymore, unfortunately
But my sunflower, however, will be ever growing,
Branches and leaves
~~Stretch marks and dead ends~~
Petals and flowers
~~Down days and days without a shower~~
A colourful personality and a purpose in life.
Flowers don't grow overnight,
and
Neither does confidence.

People can cut off your leaves, but they will always grow back,
I'm not a botanist - Christ, I can barely keep a houseplant
But if wet-the-beds can turn to wishes, you are not limited in
ambitions

Everything is still steady,
Everything is still calm,
Overthinking will be the death of me
It's just the anxiety,
It's not who I am.

Pluto

I am just the same as everybody else.

I may be

Small

But I am still relevant.

Who was Earth to decide

I am not .

We revolve around the same sun.
I received your party invite

I

Lost

It

We can all be careless sometimes.
Just because I am so far, does not mean I am not there.

Not that I want to be.

But again, dare I require a label, to be

In the lottery of existence, I was an accident,
Why choose me if I don't serve a purpose?

To be seen, not to be heard.

I exist on the outskirts of everybody else,
I have a moon,
I have a ground,
I am just the same as you,

We are different.

I wished for affection in an atmosphere of rejection.

I wear my heart on my sleeve, you can see it
Everybody can.
It just isn't enough.

It's alright, I don't think Hades has a clue what hes morphing
into either.

I can hear the voice of the underworld.

I am the voice of the underworld

I am the underworld

I am.

The Moon

Luna,
Always was my 'girls name'
I'd hoped.
But maybe I'll just get a cat again one day,
When the time is right.

People on Earth,
At least the vast majority of them,
Appreciate and connect with you most,
When you're in the light,
Out of the shadows,
Whole.
At least from Earth you are.
They rarely see you blue.
With the power to light up the sky, my love,
You are more ~~to them~~ than your beauty.
Energy controlling oceans,
A place they still don't really know,
Not as well as they ~~think they~~ know you.

It must get so lonely out here.
They made this thing called 'time' which aligns with your ways.
Can we use it to figure out your birthday?

Although, I caution you of the chaos.
We have some issues with race, religion, politicians and sexism
Since people started caring about what's in your pants and
who's in your bed
It's because it's not natural, so naturally they see red

The people's passion for protest and righteousness for wisdom
Is the only fucking hope for a future where we're ~~winning~~
living.

Luna,
There is a pleasure in my lunatic life,
Your presence.
Your persistence in the know of night and day,
I may belong a world away, though I am here for you.
To remind you,
To comfort you,
To make you proud and remind you that I need you,
To comfort me.

My love and compassion will take you to the moon and back
when you need it.
I used to be so independent and now I can't be alone without
refraining from picking up my phone
I paint you into pictures, I write you into rhyme, I still act cool
despite you're on my mind pretty much all the time
That's fine, actually better. Without realising it you deafen the
depression, the voices and suicidal lessons
I've never felt more alive so thank fuck I didn't die when I
tried because the grass really is greener on the other side.

Return

We've no got two pennies to rub together,
We keep saying it's going to get better but
It's not about what I can afford,
Sure money would help but we never get bored.
Most kiss frogs before they find their prince,
I'd been kissing snakes and venom isn't really to my taste.
-I'll take a Tennent's instead mate
Once you're treated the way you should be all of that time
before was a bit of a waste,
That's okay babe, it takes a little time and it isn't a race.
The prince and the popper but his burds a bit of a rocker
A lass with a little class and a lot of sass depending on what's
in her glass
I would take you to cloud 9 with the silver line,
But someone's already sniffed it.
There's no room for a silver spoon in the scheme,
Well there probably is but I bet it's no clean.
I've made a year clean but I canny get off the green
Higher than the price of gas on the puff, puff, pass.
we can tell which side you're on from the moment you arrive.
"Cunt" is a term of endearment here, to mothers despair
but if you start acting like one you'll be leaving with a black
eye as a token of a goodbye.
If there's gonna be a scrap you'll only cause a scene and
everyone knows everything in the scheme.
Who said romance is dead,
Rhyme
And
Poetry

Low and behold, Silvia Plath is on par with Eminem
Somewhat similar in the end, add a decent rhythm and she'd
be spitting bars but
Somehow I can't imagine that on the aux when we're smoking
in cars.
Adidas hand-me-downs and neighbours outside in dressing
gowns,
Any gaff is better than a night in the toon.
You can take the wain out of the scheme,
But we'll always be back
Wanty know why?
Because the scheme is absolutely fuckin class

DRAGON'S BLOOD
GABRIEL GONTOR

CHAPTER ONE

In the bunker below the mountain close to the village of Freezing Sun lay the lab and base of operations of Professor Abaddon.

Beyond the scorched door in the icy wasteland, lay a hulk of a man whose scaly skin is covered in ice from head to toe but with flames searing through all his joints. He is wielding a sword that seems transparent but is glowing with both the magic energies of fire and ice. The man is breathing hard with exhaustion having fought half of Abaddon's army getting to the bunker.

Abaddon himself is a tall, pale skinny man whose head is surrounded in a strange dark glow of swirling energy. He turns from his lab table to face the man in front of him and said in a tone that was both dry and smooth at the same time,

"So the famous Magnus Blaze has finally made his move, or should I call you Mighty Dragon Warrior instead?"

Abaddon's black energy swirls around his head and morphs into a smug smile.

"You are FINISHED, Abaddon!" Blaze roars, as he raises his sword ready to incinerate him. "Your evil plans will never succeed. Your army is defeated, and it is time for you to die."

Abaddon calmly walks towards the goliath of Magnus Blaze with the grace and ease of a predator who didn't want to rush his food.

Magnus raises his sword that is pulsing with fire and ice energy, thinking

'Why is he so calm? He must know he cannot escape death?'

Blaze swipes the sword towards Abaddon, the fire energy glows and erupts from the edge like lava. The ice energy shoots from the tip of the sword like blue lightning. Magnus swings the sword around his head, combining the fire and ice energies into one deadly force and with a mighty crash he plunges the sword towards the heart of Professor Abaddon. Fire and ice explode in a huge ball of blue flame that fans out destroying everything in the room.

As the building shudders, and the air clears Magnus steps forward.

"You only have yourself to blame Abaddon, I tried to reason with you" he says as he lays the sword down, totally drained of energy.

BUT where is Abaddon? There is no sign of him. No shattered bones. No blood. No charred flesh. Nothing.

Magnus stood still, unsure of what had happened. He closes his eyes and tries to feel for Abaddon's energy. Suddenly from the edge of his awareness he notices a surge of energy. Too late – as the energy pulse flows through Magnus's thoughts and seals him into a prison within his own mind. He feels his life fire dim, his body unable to respond and the world go dark as Abaddon's laughter echos in his ears.

'Nooooo', he cries silently. With his life force draining he summons every ounce of strength and sends out a beacon of thought energy to the only people who can save him and the planet.

"SOM, QUILO it is your time. Awaken to your power my sons, learn your heritage, unleash the DRAGON. The world needs YOU"

***

Taking the great Dragon's mind was so easy just like controlling all the others, thought Abaddon.

"I expected more from you, Magnus." He said as he leaned over the body of the most powerful dragon left in the world. As his human form began to change and Abaddon kicked the spikey tail that emerged from his body.

"I knew my chaos energy was more powerful. Nothing will stop me now. I can control the minds of every man and creature on the planet. Soon everyone will do my bidding."

"Ha ha Magnus! Haven't got anything to say now? No ice, no fire just locked in the darkness of your mind. Serves you right, death is too quick. I think I'll let you suffer in there. All lost and alone." Abaddon snarled as he grabbed the last man dragon's head.

Suddenly, Abaddon caught hold of the last message and image that had been captured within Magnus's energy field.

He could see two boys, one with white hair and one with black. And two powerful swords hidden within another realm. Abaddon shuddered as a vision of the future played out in front of him.

"The swords started to glow, blue ice energy of one and red fire energy of the other. The two boys grabbed the swords and they changed into dragons. They combined the energy streams flowing from the swords and a HUGE beacon of light shot upwards to the sky."

"So, you have sons, you aren't the last Dragon! You were right to hide them but don't worry Magnus – I'll look after them." Abaddon sneered.

"I'll help them to find their power and we'll be a great team. NOTHING and NO-ONE will be able to stop us once they work with me. HA HA HA!" he cackled.

"Now all I need is to find your boys. They'll be easy to control. Come to your new daddy – it's fun on the dark side".

Professor Abaddon, summoned up a circle of energy. He plucked a hair from Magnus's head and stepped into the green vortex. His body changed, his voice deepened and now stood looking exactly like Magnus Blaze.

"Hello Som and Quilo – daddy's home" he laughed as he opened a portal to another dimension.

CHAPTER TWO

Som was walking back home from school with his brother Quilo, feeling pleased it had been an accident-free day. His new schoolteachers were particularly angry with him after the second fire in the science room. He tried to explain it wasn't his fault and that things just happened. He was accident-prone that was all, but he had been warned the school would call his parents in if there were any more incidents. *Good luck with that*, he thought *Mum's always busy and who knows where Dad is?*

As they walked down the hill to their house at the bottom, the only one that didn't have the paint fading or peeling off.

Som asked Quilo "Do you think that Dad could find us here?"

but Quilo didn't even bother to answer as he was completely engrossed in his mystery book.

As the boys reached the front gate, Som saw his mum on a makeshift ladder of loosely tied together planks of wood painting the side of the house. She looked happy, with her amber hair tied back in a bun and a white scarf covering her head. Som had a strange feeling in his stomach that she was going to fall off and leapt over the fence and grabbed the ladder.

"Hey Mum, what's for lunch?" he asked.

"Help me down first and you'll find out" as her feet touched the ground she said "thanks Som I wasn't sure how much longer that ladder was going to last."

She headed into the house through the pitch-black door with strange symbols engraved in various colours. The brothers followed her in and as Som felt his stomach grumble he noticed the same symbols and circles etched into all the doors. "Why do you do this in every house we move to Mum?"

"You know I just like these designs. They make me feel safe. Now get the chicken salad out of the fridge while I wash my hands, please." Mum shouted as she climbed the stairs to the bathroom.

"Quilo, don't you think this is odd? What's this all about?" Som asked as he pulled food from the fridge.

"I don't know. She's always done it! Maybe it's got something to do with Dad?

She won't talk about him. I've been asking her lots of questions, but she just changes the subject" Quilo replied as he grabbed a piece of chicken.

"I want to know where he is, and I think I have found some clues".

"What, where how?" Som spluttered.

"I found some letters hidden in mum's wardrobe. Dad's been writing to her all this time. I read something about it's time for us to know".

"Time for us to know what?"

"I don't know but Mum almost caught me, so I didn't finish reading. I'm going to try again later" said Quilo. "If we could get her to go out then we can search."

"Yeah, that sounds that sounds like a good plan," Som responded with a mouth full of food.

"It's time for me to do my homework - see you at dinner time," he says as he swallows his food and goes to the kitchen to grab an apple then disappears upstairs.

***

"Quilo what are you doing" Som said to his brother as he saw him rifling through various multi-coloured letters he had pulled from under the floor beside their mum's closet.

"I wonder why all these letters have weird symbols on them do you think it means something Som? Get over here." said Quilo from the other side of the room, crouching and motioning to Som with icy blue gloves and as sunlight bathed his cold pale body. As Som drew nearer he noticed that his brother had bags under his eyes and that his icy blue hair and eyes were turning paler.

Som was worried about Quilo, ever since he first found these letters, he was obsessed with finding their dad. He wasn't sleeping or eating properly and seemed a bit spaced out.

Quilo focused on the letter, almost looking through it, like he was finally starting to see what was in front of him. Then as he flipped over the letter, he saw something odd - a faintly glowing symbol, it had two curved lines at opposite ends.

"I think these are part of a spell circle." Som couldn't explain how he knew this. "I think it's dangerous, we need to be really careful". As he stood up, he saw his brother stare intensely out of the window.

"Look Som, it's Dad" Quilo shouted, "he's found us, he's come home to us at last".

Som looked out of the window and saw the outline of a man walking towards the house, but something didn't feel right. Som's eyes started to burn with fire, his skin prickled with heat and started to glow.

Quilo opened the window and climbed out. Som tried to grab him, but he shook him off.

"I need to see him. Dad, Dad – I'm coming" shouted Quilo.

Quilo dropped to the ground and ran towards the figure as Som screamed, "I think we should wait till mum is back. Don't do anything reckless. There is something we are missing.'"

But Quilo kept running as if in a trance.

CHAPTER THREE

Walking on the sidewalk Abaddon saw a house that had some weird protection symbols that he hadn't seen before. "So, this is where you are hiding!" he muttered to himself.

As he prowled closer, he saw a boy in a blue hoodie looking out the window. He had a cold completion and staring ice eyes that reminded Abaddon of Magnus Blaze. "This is going to be easy" he said as he started to send his mind control energy towards the boy.

"Come closer, come to DADDY!" Abaddon smirked under his breath. He watched the lad jump from the window, land on the ground, and start to run towards him.

As the Ice Boy got closer shouting, "Dad – It's me, Quilo" Abaddon cast a spell and opened a portal door with a swirl of black and purple mist.

A small spark of blue flame lit in Quilo's eyes as he saw the portal. Ice formed on his skin and hands as he realised something was wrong, but he was too late. Abaddon laughed as he grabbed the boy and pulled him into the black doorway and the two figures vanished without leaving a trace.

Som screamed, "Nooo – Quilo" as sparks of fire flew from his body and a huge ball of red energy exploded around him sending him flying.

***

Som woke up feeling strange. His head hurt, his eyes were stinging and everything round him is blinding white - the ceiling, the floor, and the walls. He was no longer wearing his favourite red hoody and gloves but had on a white cloth suit.

"Am I dead? Where am I?"

Suddenly a door opened, and a dark silhouette appeared in the space. As he entered the room, Som's eyes focussed on a large man wearing dark armour. He had a mop of curly silver white hair that stood out against his grey complexion. His nose looked slightly bent on the side like it had been broken and not set right and his face came to an angular point at his chin.

"Ah you are awake; I'm going to have to take that nap off your house score. 10 points ought to do it." as he tapped something onto a screen then winked. He then said in an accusing tone "why aren't you ready? You have class in 10 minutes do you want to lose more points."

Som slid back on to the pillow, thinking *"I must be dreaming or have gone crazy"*

A rounder smiling man entered the room "Let *me* explain everything".

"Don't worry you are safe. Your mum found you and called us to help. I am sorry Som, we have let you and Quilo down. We thought it was best to protect you, but we should have realised he could find you".

"Who? What happened? Where's Mum and Quilo? asked Som, feeling even more confused.

"You are at the Forrest School of Magic. I'm Simon, a professor here and a friend of your mum's. She is fine, she is out looking for Quilo."

"You had a bit of an accident, there was a fire. You kept telling your mum that Quilo had gone with Dad. But we think both your dad and Quilo are in danger. We think Professor Abaddon has them".

Som's memory flashed back to him. "I saw Quilo disappear with a man. He looked like Dad but there was something wrong. Who is Professor Abaddon?"

"Abaddon was a professor at the school here, but he always wanted to challenge the order of things. He wants to open the veil between all worlds and have access to the darkest magic. With this he would be unstoppable." Simon explained. "He developed his mind control powers here. He was thrown out of the school when he took over the school principals mind and forced her to give him access to the magic vaults of all knowledge."

"But what has this got to do with me?" asked Som

"Your Dad, Magnus Blaze is the most powerful dragon left in the world. He sealed the veil so Abaddon could not open it. Magnus hid his powers in his sons – you and Quilo. Fire and Ice together are powerful energies and can break the strongest of spells. If Abaddon can control this, then we are lost."

"Your mum has been moving you boys around to keep you safe, but something changed. Abaddon found out about you. We think he has your dad and your brother in his control".

"It's all too much" Som cried. "So, this is why I set things on fire? I am a Dragon?"

"Quit your blubbering" says a girl with dark skin, bright red and gold hair that almost looked like it was on fire. Her crimson eyes, held a defiant look as she glared at Som. "I'm Noelle, you need to learn to control your magic quickly. There's a lot at stake and I'm going to teach you. So, get up and follow me and if you learn fast, you can even get lunch".

"Food, now your talking – I'm starving!" Som, wiped his eyes, got up and followed her.

As Som went out of the bright white room and into an arched hallway with Byzantine mosaics covering all the walls and ceilings. One caught his attention; it was a picture of two warriors in leather armour and they had a weapon in one hand and fire in the other. Som felt the power radiating from the Mosaic, he looked for Noelle and noticed she was halfway down the corridor already.

"STOP" Som shouted and surprisingly she froze as if she couldn't move at all.

As Som ran to Noelle something caught his attention. Out of the corner of his eye he saw smoke. He spun around and saw a boy, lying on the ground covered in rubble. He was cut and bleeding. There were flames everywhere and he could hear people screaming. Som started to panic and felt fear well up inside his stomach, he scrunched his hands into a ball and screamed as sparks emerged from his fingers.

Suddenly, Noelle grabbed him "hey, what's going on?"

Som jumped and opened his eyes, the corridor was clear. No smoke, no flames and no one screaming.

"Where did he go?" he asked. "What's happening?"

"Where did who go?" Noelle asked.

"I saw a boy; he was badly hurt. The walls were on top of him, and people were screaming. It was so real and scary."

"Oh no – it's starting! We need to tell the Principal; she'll know what to do" Noelle grabbed Som and started to run to the school office.

Principal Levyo opened the door. "Come in Sssom" her voice trailing in a slight hissing sound. "I know this mussst be confusssing and ssscary for you. But tell me what you sssaw?"

Som repeated the story as he stared into her hypnotic eyes.

"You have had a visssion of the future. We need to fassst track your learning. We are all in grave danger. Abaddon'sss powersss are growing now he hasss your brother with him. He will be coming for you sssoon."

The Principal turned to Noelle "Go and ssset up the training arena. Sssom will have to learn to fight. He needsss to unleasssh hisss magic to find the fire sssword."

***

Som thought the boy standing opposite him looked familiar.

"I'm Derik" he said stretching out his hand. "I'm going to train you to use some weapons".

"That's cool" Som walked into the arena circle as a red barrier erected itself around the perimeter of the circle trapping him inside. A section of the floor in front of him rises in a semi-circle to surround him with weapons.

He moved toward the swords, drawn by slim and silvery looking traditional Chinese sword.

"Is this a Jian gentleman's sword?"

"Yes", said Derik "it's very rare. So, you like swords then?"

"I've always had a thing for swords. The principal said I must find the Fire Sword. Is it here?"

"Yes and no" Derik shrugged. "I've never seen it. It's supposed to be hidden in the school somewhere with the Ice Sword. But the legend is that only the most powerful dragons can find and activate them."

"I've just been told that my dad is a dragon. I didn't know, he looked normal to me, but I haven't seen him for so long. It's all so confusing." Som shrugged.

"I'm ready to learn who I really am."

With that, he turned and saw two daggers also Chinese in origin called butterfly blades. As he grabbed the daggers, he felt a surge of energy flow through his body. A sheath for the sword had appeared on his back and decorative sheaths for the daggers had appeared at each side of his waist. Gauntlets formed on his hands, and he felt ready for anything.

The armoury retracted back into the ground, and he saw Noelle standing in the middle of the circle watching him. She was wearing a pair of silver gauntlets inlayed with metal that glowed a faint red. She also had a breast plate inlayed with red and combat boots with metal plating all over her lower legs.

Derik walked towards Som. "You can control these weapons, not only with your hands but also with your energy. Noelle is going to fight you; you need to believe in your abilities. Use your fire energy."

"I don't want to hurt her"

"Ha you won't get near me" laughed Noelle "just watch you don't get hurt pretty boy!"

Noelle stood with her arms raised and her legs apart. Som took one step towards her with his sword raised in one hand and a dagger in the other.

He lashed out with the sword, sure he would strike Noelle, but she disappeared leaving a flickering flame where she was standing just a second ago.

Som suddenly sensed a heat behind his head before he went flying into the barrier. His vision went dark and all he could think of was *that has got to be a joke I can't die yet* as everything disappeared, and he was engulfed in fire.

As the fire swirled around his body completely encasing him, he heard a deep ancient sounding voice.

"You are finally here, the saviour of the dimension and my soon to be master Som"

Som replied "I am nobodies master I can't even fight back. I have no power, so it is best if you forget about me. I am not master material all I want is to find my brother and go home. If I can't beat Noelle then I can't save dad and Quilo"

As if on cue, the fire surrounding Som started to take shape and mould itself into an outline of his body, taking on a lifeforce of its own.

"Do I look powerless to you?" it boomed.

Som realised the fire was a reflection of him. That its power was his power and that he could get stronger. He closed his eyes and accepted the fire into him. It was changing him, making his muscles tougher, his mind sharper and every part of his body began to grow scales as black as night. His teeth sharpened like sharks. White circular marks started to appear all over him starting at his toes then swirling around his feet, hands, forehead, and chest. Around his heart a hollow circle appeared with a flame in the centre and on his head is an outline of a flower with four petals. He felt the burning sensation pulsing through his veins. He took a deep breath surging with fire energy and opened his eyes.

Som was back in the arena. Noelle was in front of him, she charged towards him but Som could see what she was going to do, everything was moving in slow motion and before she was even halfway to him he moved behind her. Noelle sensed his new power and exploded with pure flame energy, as it coated her body, she wasn't in slow motion anymore but still wasn't fast enough to match him. As she started her attack, he could dodge every strike without thinking.

Som raised his sword, in one swift motion almost catching her but she managed to stop the momentum by punching the flat end of the sword. As she grabbed it and hit him with a hard punch, the sword shattered.

Som leapt over Noelle and kicked the back of her knees. With one push he pinned her down, holding one butterfly blade in-between her shoulder blades and one under her chin. "It is over" he said and Noelle nodded.

Derik rushed over "wow, what happened to you? That was amazing – no one can beat Noelle."

"I found my true self. My inner dragon fire has been opened. But boy do I need something to eat now!" Som collapsed exhausted.

CHAPTER FOUR

baddon laughed as Quilo followed him through the portal. "Stupid boy, so easily fooled by a cloaking spell and a little mind control magic. Now you can help me to find your brother and destroy your father. Then are going to have fun – look out world here we come"

Quilo sat dazed and withdrawn, his eyes shone with a bright blue ice fire, but he was trapped inside his own mind. As his own thoughts faded, slipping away like water down a drain, he focussed on a picture of his brother *"Som help me, I'm sorry"*.

Abaddon walked over towards Magnus Blaze who was in his true dragon form lying curled up in the corner of a dark, cold stone room.

"Look who I've brought home for tea" he laughed. "This is all much easier that I thought. Your wife managed to take Som but don't worry. I'll find them soon and when I do – it's all over. No one will stop me."

Magnus stared at his son Quilo, a small tear escaped from his eye and rolled down his scaley cheek. He couldn't move, still powerless under the dark magic of Abaddon, but there was a little spark of fire in the dark recess of his mind. *"I'm not gone yet boys, together we can still save the world. Hurry Som find the Fire Sword and break the spell*" he sent the thought out through the stone walls hoping it would find his only hope.

***

Som, was almost inhaling the pizza. "I'm soooo hungry, fighting takes a lot of energy"

Derik and Noelle laughed together. "We hadn't noticed!"

As Som took the last slice from the plate he felt a strange surge of heat energy and found himself in a huge room filled with books. Two stone columns were in front of him with a small green door in the middle. It had an image of a dragon carved into the wood and two swords crossed over his head. "*Hurry Som find the Fire Sword and break the spell*" a voice said as the books disappeared, and he was back sitting at the table.

Noelle touched his arm "Are you ok? Your skin was glowing, and you went all weird for a minute"

"Is there a book room here?"

"Of course, there is a library, it's a school dummy!" said Derik.

"We need to go now; I think the Fire Sword is there" Som was already on his feet.

"Follow us" shouted Derik as he started to run.

The Librarian came running as the three friends crashed through the door.

"What's going on? Calm down you three"

"Where's the green door with the dragon?" asked Som.

"There's no green door in here"

"There must be. I saw it. It's between two stone pillars" Som spun around the huge space.

"Where are the books on Dragons?" Noelle asked.

"Follow me" and the Librarian walked down a long corridor, through heavy double doors, around a corner and led the trio to a small turret room in the corner of the library. "This is our dragon collection"

Som walked into the turret. "I am a Dragon, son of Magus Blaze and I'm here to find the Fire Sword"

Suddenly his head was swimming, the turret started to move, books were flying off the shelves as two stone columns rose out of the floor and a green door magically appeared in front of them.

"Wow, said the Librarian, "I've never seen this before".

Derik and Noelle looked at each other. "We better tell the principal; I'll go shouted Derik and he ran out of the room.

All at once a shrill alarm was ringing out and people started to run out of the library.

"The school's perimeter has been breached. We are in danger" the Librarian tried to pull Noelle out with him, but she stood her ground.

"No, we need to help Som. If Abaddon gets in, we are all doomed" she shouted.

But before either of them could move Som placed his hand on the door.

Strange carvings appeared in the wood - a dragon, two swords and several rune symbols.

Som recognised the symbols as the same ones his mum painted on every house, they lived in. "This is it. The Sword must be here" as he tried to pull open the door.

No matter how hard he pulled the door would not move. The door was still protected. The carvings glowed and Som remembered his mum singing the same song over and over to Quilo and him. **Dragon's blood of ice and fire, open up your heart's desire, only when the time is right, will your body stand and fight, if the world is at an end, unleash your powers to defend"**

As he repeated the words and placed both hands on the door, it opened wide revealing a room bursting with bright crystal energy and in the centre stood two huge silver swords glowing with fire and ice. Som raced towards the fire sword and grabbed it with both hands.

Fire surged through his veins, he felt as though his body would tear apart. He looked at his hands as his gloves transformed into scaled gauntlets, soon his whole body was covered in a green, pearlescent armour.

Suddenly the building shook and the noise of an explosion rang in Som's ears.

Walls started to crack, large blocks of masonry falling, books flying everywhere, as he heard the shouts and cries of pupils and teachers. The air was thick with smoke and dust.

"Quick Som, this way" Noelle screamed at him.

"I need to get the other sword first. I think Quilo needs this." Som grabbed the ice sword, it hissed in his hands. He strapped it to his back and followed Noelle.

They ran out of the library and along the corridor. Another explosion ripped the building as more walls collapsed. Som looked ahead and saw someone covered in rubble. As they got closer, he recognised Derik, lying groaning in the debris, blood dripping from his head.

"No - it's all coming true. Abaddon is here. Derik please be ok" Som sat down beside his new friend.

The principal, and senior teachers arrived. "Quick Sssssom, we need to fight. Ssssomeone will help Derik. Abaddon and his army are here and Quilo is with him. We need you"

Noelle pulls Som with her as they start to run toward the sound of fighting.

They enter the main hall and see teachers and pupils fighting Abaddon's goons. But just as soon as they strike the enemy, an energy burst rushes through the hall knocking everyone over.

"MUM?" Som looks astonished to see his mother, run into the room. She is wearing purple armour and carrying a large, pointed spear like weapon, her long hair flowing behind her.

"SOM, I'm so happy to see you. Sorry, there's a lot to explain but now we need to fight. Have you seen Quilo?"

"No, I think he is close, but his energy feels different. Mum – WE ARE DRAGONS???"

"YES, you are, and isn't this the lovely family gathering!" shouted a man's voice.

Abaddon stood laughing. "This is even better than I hoped. Now I can control all of you at once"

Som's mum and other teachers surround Abaddon. "We are not giving up easily" she shouts. "Run Som - find Quilo".

Noelle and Som run out of the hall and spot Quilo fighting a teacher. Noelle leads the charge and hits Quilo with bolts of energy. He fights back with ice, sending Noelle flying into a wall.

"QUILO STOP!" Som shouts as he rushes towards him brandishing his Fire Sword. Quilo throws ice energy at Som and he deflects hearing a hiss as fire and ice meet.

"I don't want to hurt you, please Quilo" shouts Som as he lashes out with his sword. Quilo is stunned but keeps fighting.

Suddenly Noelle appears and casts a fire spell while Som hits him with a huge bolt from the sword at the same time. Quilo rocks on his heels and falls over, hitting his head on the floor.

"What's going on? SOM? Where am I?" Quilo rubbed his head and looked around him.

"Quilo, thank goodness you are ok." Noelle helped him to his feet. "There's soo much to explain but you were under Abaddon's spell. The fall and fire energy hit must have broken it."

Som hugged his twin brother. "Do you know where Dad is? Abaddon has him locked up somewhere and we need to save him."

"It's all a bit fuzzy" Quilo rubbed his head. "I'm sorry if I hurt you. I couldn't stop it."

"That's ok – we Dragons are tough!"

"Dragons????? What are you talking about Som?"

"We are Dragons, so is Dad. That's why we have all this weird stuff going on." Som grabbed his sword and it pulsed with fire. "See – I have fire energy and you have ice energy."

"Great guys, time for family catch ups later." Said Noelle "If we don't defeat Abaddon and save your dad, the whole world is in danger. COME ON we need to help the others."

"Take this ice sword Quilo, it belongs to you" shouted Som "think of Dad and activate all your power."

Quilo held the heavy sword in both hands and felt the energy rise from the ground. His sword started to glow ice blue but it faded quickly.

"You need to connect your heart energy. Think of your dad" Noelle encouraged.

Som looked at Quilo and grabbed his arm "Remember him playing with us at Christmas when we were younger. He gave us swords and we fought in the garden with him."

"I remember" Quilo said as he held his sword above his head. "I'm sorry Dad, I let you down but I'm coming to save you."

Quilo's eyes, shone with bright blue fire as the sword sparked into life. The ice energy was flowing with ice sparks flying from the tip as steel gauntlets and armour formed on his body.

"RIGHT – LET'S END THIS NOW!" shouted Noelle, as she ran towards the sound of fighting.

Som and Quilo followed Noelle, running past people bleeding and moaning. "MUM" shouted Quilo, as he saw her helping an injured man.

"Thank goodness you are ok" she said, hugging him. "It's up to you two now.

Abaddon is too strong. You and Som need to work together."

Suddenly the room grew dark, clouds formed at the ceiling and lightning sparked and a fierce wind rushed around the room as Abaddon appeared.

"You are all weak, bow to your master and I will let you live" he shouted.

"Quilo NOW" Som jumped in front of Abaddon and threw all the fire energy he could muster at Abaddon. Quilo stood at Som's side and fired ice energy from his sword. The streams of energy joined together with a HUGE explosion. Ice and fire rained down on Abaddon freezing him inside a bubble of fire.

Noelle joined the dragon boys and cast a spell towards Abaddon.

BANG! Light exploded and building shook as Som and Quilo were blown off their feet. "Where is he?" shouted Som. Abaddon had disappeared and only a smouldering pile of ash remained.

"Is he dead? Did we kill him?" asked Quilo.

"I don't know" Noelle replied "but we need to know for sure."

"Quick Som, come with me. I know there is a portal back to Abaddon's lair where Dad is. Run, we need to go now." Quilo ran towards the field outside the school with Som trailing after him.

"Please be careful," shouted their mum.

"This way, grab on to me," Quilo panted as they reached the trees at the edge of the field. "It's here, stand on the black rock. Be ready – it's a quick way to travel."

Som and Quilo stepped on to the large black rock and disappeared.

"I feel sick," retched Som, "that was horrible."

"Yeah, it's worse than the fairground rides," replied Quilo as he stood up "I'm so dizzy."

As their eyes adjusted to the dim light, they could make out a doorway and heard shuffling noises. "Sshh! It might be him" Quilo crept towards the door with his sword raised above his head. He pushed the door, it creaked as he edged his way through it. Som followed and gasped as he looked into the eyes of a dragon, curled up on the stone floor of a large metal cage.

"Dad!" Som and Quilo rushed towards the injured dragon. "It's us, we are here for you. Please be ok."

With a huge effort, Magnus Blaze the mighty dragon lifted his head, "my boys, my boys ...I knew you'd come."

"Where's Abaddon, Dad?"

"He just left, he took a part of my tail and a big box of black crystals and vanished through a portal. He's very dangerous now. We need to stop him."

"We will, but you need to rest. There's so much you need to tell us," said Som as he smashed the metal cage with his sword. "I can't believe we are dragons, it's AWESOME."

"I'm sorry Som, Quilo. I thought I was protecting you, but I put you both in danger. Let's go home, your mum will be worried sick."

"It's ok Dad, together we will be even stronger, and we'll stop Abaddon for good." Quilo helped Magnus up and led him back towards the portal.

"Hurry up, I'm starving," laughed Som. "Do you think Mum will make us pizza and chocolate cake? Saving the world is hungry work."